2

VERY SHORT
STORIES

Helen Keeling-Marston

First variant first published in 2017
Second variant first published in 2023 by Purple Pangolin Press

ISBN 978-1-3999-5794-6

For mum, dad and Colin

FOREWORD

Just as I'd got back up to speed with where the story was heading, I nodded off.

I decided to write this book because many of us don't have as much time as we'd like to read, and it can often take us weeks, or even months, to conquer a novel – and a lot of that time is spent trying to remember *what happened in chapter three, again?* So I reasoned that there was a need for a book that contained a collection of stories each so short that the reader would be able to start…and finish…a whole one in one night – some even in a minute! I hope you enjoy them.

1

As I stared into his deep blue eyes, I knew that he was 'the one'. The identity parade was over.

2

Cynicism kills magic, so while the children all knew that I existed, their parents didn't. So the parents would pretend to be me. But they never did it very well.

* * * * *

Nine-year-old Flora carefully placed the molar underneath her pillow, then quickly fell asleep. A couple of hours later, her father crept into her room, lifted her pillow and exchanged her tooth for a pound coin. Then, as he left her room, I flew in, took the pound coin and swapped it for a piece of enchanted plastic that would glow for a good few hours.

When Flora woke the next morning, she peeled back her pillow and gasped when she saw the glowing disc.

"Did the tooth fairy leave you anything?" asked Flora's mum as the family sat down to breakfast that morning.

"She did," said Flora, her eyes glowing like the disc. "She left me a coin that sparkled with fairy dust."

As Flora's parents exchanged bemused, cynical glances, I counted how much money I'd made that evening.

I never said that magic had to be used for good.

3

He'd conjured up a hauntingly beautiful tune that had been a hit across the whole of the world, so when he won the public vote for *Best Artist,* the award organisers didn't know what to do. *Could* a humpback whale win a Grammy?

4

Each of you had your good points, which is why I needed all four of you. I hope that was okay.

Number one – unlike some of the others, you were less extreme, although you had your moments. I loved how you made me feel so hopeful.

Number two – you brought such warmth into my life, which I loved you for, but you could be so intense that at times I had to get away from you.

Number three – like number one, your personality was steady and calming. However, you could also be so colourful you would take my breath away.

Number four – you challenged me the most, and you could be inhospitable and cold – too cold – but you had an interesting intensity to you.

I did try being monogamous for a few years, spending all of my time with number two – summer – but it made my life so samey, I moved back to a country that had spring, summer, autumn and winter.

5

On seeing the young girl, Ben ran up to her and gave her a high-five, and her parents beamed.

On seeing another young girl, Chris – who wasn't at all 'with it' after a heavy drinking session the night before – ran up to her and high-fived her. However, *her* parents glared at Chris and pushed him away.

* * * * *

Ben approached the policeman and tried to knock off his hat, and the policeman was a good sport about it, staging a comedy fall.

Chris approached another policeman and tried to knock off his hat. However, *this* policeman glared at Chris and told him it was an offence to disrespect a public official.

* * * * *

On spotting the elderly couple, Ben grabbed a rose from the nearby flower stall and presented it to the old lady.

"How lovely," cooed the lady while her husband smiled, appreciatively, at Ben.

On spotting another elderly couple, Chris grabbed a rose from the nearby flower stall and presented it to his couple's old lady. However, *Chris's* old lady's husband punched Chris on the nose.

* * * * *

Ben swiped the bucket from out of the woman's hand and ran around encouraging people to throw in some coins.

After an impressive display of public benevolence, Ben gave the – now much heavier – bucket back to the grateful charity collector.

Chris swiped the bucket from out of another woman's hand, but *this* woman shouted at Chris while grabbing him and pinning him to the ground. When Chris explained that he'd just wanted to collect some money for the woman's charity, the woman told Chris she wasn't born yesterday.

* * * * *

That night, as Ben and Chris sat in the pub, drinking and chatting, Chris was feeling bruised – physically and emotionally.

"The people love you. They don't me. I'm just not as good at it as you are, Ben."

"You are, mate," reassured Ben. "However, you made one big mistake today."

"What was that?" asked Chris, eager to hear Ben's reply.

"Well, the thing is, Chris," began Ben, struggling to stifle a grin. "The thing is, Chris, a good mascot doesn't usually forget to wear his costume."

6

I wanted to do well for myself, but I also wanted to do well for her. I wanted to make her proud.

It was a highly competitive race in which I took the lead, then he did, then I did, and then he did. Ultimately, however, *I* crossed the line first. *I* was victorious.

I looked up at her. She was standing on the bridge with her brother, laughing and gloating. I'd made her happy. That was good.

I wasn't a bad old stick.

7

"You have real talent and could go far in ballet, Molly," said Mr Young after six-year-old Molly performed a perfect pirouette. Molly smiled.

You have real talent and could go far in ballet, Bella, thought Mrs Banks after six-year-old Bella performed a perfect pirouette.

* * * * *

Twenty-four-year-old Molly was buzzing after her portrayal of Giselle at the Royal Opera House.

Twenty-four-year-old Bella thoroughly enjoyed watching Molly Sanderson play Giselle at the Royal Opera House, and she dreamt that it had been her up there on the stage.

8

"There's going to be a storm soon."

"How do you know, grandma?"

"Because my knees hurt."

I loved my grandma – she was so random.

"Grandma's probably right," said my mum, who was a doctor. "When there's a storm on the horizon, the atmospheric pressure drops, so the sensory nerve endings in grandma's knees are currently experiencing an increase in fluid pressure that's causing them to hurt. That's how she can predict the weather."

Further proof that she's Supergran, I thought, contentedly.

9

"Take the job. You're ready. Just go for it."

"But do you really think I'm ready? Maybe I should wait until I've got a few more years' experience?"

"No, you have enough experience now. Go for it. An opportunity like this might never come along again."

"But surely it will? And that opportunity might be a better opportunity, and I'd have more experience."

"I doubt it. Opportunities like these are once-in-a-lifetime. Miss out now, miss out forever."

"But that's such fatalistic thinking. Other opportunities always come along."

"No, this is your one and only chance. You can't let it pass you by."

"But I'm not good enough."

"What an attitude! Have you thought about maybe believing in yourself?"

"But what if I fail? What if I completely and utterly mess up?"

"You won't. Think about your past endeavours that turned out to be successful, even though you thought you'd mess up them, too."

"I guess, but…"

"But what? Running out of excuses now, aren't you?"

"But what if I go for it, get out of my depth and end up crippled with stress?"

"But what if you don't go for it, don't get out of your depth and end up crippled with boredom?"

"You're quite annoying, aren't you?"

"No, *I'm* not annoying – *you're* annoying."

"Can one person be both annoying and not annoying?"

10

I'd never seen so many tigers before. You'd think I'd have been scared, but they were just cubs, and they seemed harmless enough. So I walked through them – a little wary, a little cautious.

Boom! One was on my back. Oh my. Now I was in for it. I didn't feel any pain, though. The tiger had wrapped its limbs around my neck and waist, but it seemed as though it just wanted to play. So I walked around with it on my back for a while – not an inconsiderable weight – then carefully placed it back down on the ground and it ran off. *Phew. That had been a close call.* I continued on my way.

Just as I was nearing where I was wanting to get to, I was attacked again, but this time by a clown. How I hated clowns; they'd really spooked me out when I was a child. This clown jumped onto my front and started to kiss me. It seemed as if it knew me, and maybe I knew it too; it was hard to tell given all of its face paint. I put him – or her – down, then took my final, purposeful steps towards the bar.

How I hated children's parties.

11

Living was pretty incredible really.

You realised this when faced with the fact that you might not be doing much more of it.

We knew it was bad because the ashen-faced cabin crew kept exchanging fearful looks. This wasn't just turbulence.

"This is your captain speaking. Prepare for an emergency landing in the sea. Brace for impact. Brace for impact."

While thinking that properly watching the emergency

drill would have been a good idea, I grabbed the seat in front of me and told my wife to do the same, then I slipped one of my hands into hers.

"Is that a good idea?" she gasped.

"Did you know," I began, "that sea otters hold hands when they sleep so they won't drift apart."

12

As the footballer prepared to take the penalty, he thought back to what his friend, the neurosurgeon, had said.

"When moving around the matter, I know that if I stray into the region known as 'the eloquent brain', I could permanently damage, or disable, my patient."

That was pressure.

13

"How does it work?" asked Simon, holding the thermometer.

"When it gets warmer, the particles in the mercury move more and take up more space, so the liquid rises up the tube and displays a higher temperature."

"Wow," said Simon. "I didn't know that things got bigger when they got warmer."

"Yes. Remember how we went to Paris last year and saw the Eiffel Tower?"

"Yes, we had ice creams at the bottom."

"Yes, that's right, we did."

"I had a mint ice cream."

"Yes, I think you did. And, if I remember correctly, mine was toffee-flavoured and mummy's was vanilla. Well, anyway, during the summer, the Eiffel Tower can be up to fifteen centimetres taller than it is in winter."

"Wow," said Simon, before furrowing his brow and appearing to be deep in thought. "So, if I'd have left my ice cream in the heat for a while, would it have got bigger and would I have had more ice cream?"

"Nice idea," laughed Simon's dad, "but it doesn't quite work like that."

14

He was single, and he really wanted to meet a lady. Yet whenever he went on dates, his legs would turn to jelly and he would shake. The final straw came this one time; a time when he was sure that this particular date was going well. But his date started weeping, so he blew a raspberry and she punched him. So, from that day forth, he never tried to woo another lady again.

The lady took her receipt.

Single Cream 300ML – £1.19
Pink Lady Apple Minimum 5 Pack – £2.50
Soft Pitted Dates 250G – £2.00
Strawberry Jelly – £0.54
Chocolate Milkshake 4x200ML – £1.60
Drinking Straws 120 Pack – £1.00
Dried Thyme 16G – £0.70
Dried Thyme 16G – £0.70
Soft Pitted Dates 250G – £2.00
Well Fired Loaf 400G – £1.00
Soft Pitted Dates 250G – £2.00
Everyday Value Regular Tissues 225S – £0.65
Raspberries 150G – £2.00
Heavy Duty Hole Punch – £5.00
Day Cream SPF 15 70ML – £15.00

Woo Woo Cocktail 250ML – £1.79
Pink Lady Apple Minimum 5 Pack – £2.50

Keith, the student, made up lots of stories at the checkout that summer.

15

"Did you hear how the humans have copied us?" said Mrs Gecko to Mr Gecko.

"No, do tell."

"They realised that our feet are covered in thousands of tiny elastic hairs that allow us to stick to surfaces, so they've developed gloves that are covered in tiny hairs that allow them to scale walls."

16

Walter was a salesman.

Will was a time traveller.

One day, Walter knocked on Will's door.

"Good day to you, sir. My name's Walter Carlton."

"Will," replied the young time traveller.

"Tell me, Will," said Walter. "Have you ever wanted to know why onions make us cry? And would you be surprised to know that the surface area of Russia is greater than the surface area of Pluto?"

Not the new milkman, then, thought Will.

"And if I told you that your sneezes could reach speeds of up to 100 miles an hour, would you be blown away?"

Will didn't know what to say. Some days were just so random. Even for a time traveller.

"Well, young Will," continued Walter, "if you're keen

to learn more fascinating facts like these, may I recommend you purchase Grayton's Global Encyclopaedia?"

"Ah, I see," said Will, the penny dropping.

"Grayton's Global Encyclopaedia is the world's greatest learning tool and the library that never closes," chirruped Walter. "Its general index makes it easy for you to find whatever information you're looking for – and what home wouldn't want to boast such a smart-looking set of books?"

What home indeed, thought Will.

"Grayton's Global Encyclopaedia…" began Walter.

"…will one day go from taking up a whole shelf's worth of space to taking up no space at all," finished Will.

Walter, as Brighton's top Grayton's Global Encyclopaedia salesman, wasn't used to having his patter punctuated; especially by such lunacy. So, for once, he was lost for words. "No…no space?" he stammered.

"That's right," said Will. "One day, nearly all households will own a computer, or multiple computers, and these computers will form a huge network called *the Internet* that will enable a computer to communicate with any other computer. What's more, there will be something called the World Wide Web, which will allow information to be accessed over the medium of the Internet. And, thanks to the Internet and the World Wide Web, people will be able to access any information, or facts, that they desire through their computers – some of which will be smaller than the palms of their hands."

"Madman," muttered Walter under his breath before scurrying away for his own safety.

17

Grandpa Roberts watched his young grandson with fascination. Chai's thumb was working its way around the phone at ferocious speed.

"It's a brave new world, that's for sure," mused Grandpa Roberts, marvelling at the mobile phone.

"Although the world's also older than it's ever been, grandpa," replied Chai.

18

"I before e, except after c," said the tutor.

The pigeon fancier scratched his head.

19

As Heidi was saying goodbye to her daughter, another parent, Lisa, was at the other end of the playground saying goodbye to her son. Heidi glanced over at Lisa and envied her tall, sinewy frame, and Lisa turned to look in Heidi's direction and smiled as she caught Heidi's eye. How she wished that she was as petite as Heidi.

Lisa saw Heidi suddenly scrabbling around in her bag, searching for her pulsating phone, and she had a flashback to the exciting and fast-paced career that she'd once had, pre-children.

Heidi put the phone to her ear and endured the wrath of her boss; a boss who often forgot that some of his staff were also doing their bit to further the human race. As she let the torrent of abuse go in one ear and out the other, she looked back over at Lisa, who was chatting to one of the other parents about taking their younger children to the park for the day.

Lisa fastened her younger son into his car seat and drove out of the nursery school car park, and she hadn't gone very far when her car made a disconcerting crunching sound and ground to a halt. She punched the steering wheel in frustration. *Stupid old banger.* Heidi, not realising that it was Lisa in the broken-down vehicle, drove past in her new 4x4, wondering whether she should sell the 4x4 and go part-time so she could spend more time with her daughter.

20

'Keeping up with the Joneses' was what they called it. When one neighbour had something done to their house, the other had to follow suit. Yet these weren't just ten-a-penny houses. They were castles.

When Tom dug a moat around his castle, Graham had to dig one too. Then, when Graham extended his castle by adding a new east wing, Tom added a new east wing too.

That evening, the sea washed both Tom's and Graham's castles away.

21

Daedalus needed to escape from the labyrinth in Crete – and fast – as giving Ariadne the thread had put him in grave danger. However, he had no idea how he was going to get himself, and his son, out of the maze and off the island. He was flummoxed.

The answer came to him in a dream about a flock of birds. They needed *wings*. Wings would propel them up and out of the labyrinth, and then they could fly to the safety of another land.

So Daedalus set about crafting two sets of wings, using wax and feathers as his raw materials.

Once the wings were complete, Daedalus gave his son, Icarus, some ground rules.

"Whatever you do, don't fly too close to the sea, or you might clog up your feathers with salt; and don't fly too close to the sun."

Icarus had always had trouble hearing, but was sure that he'd heard properly, and understood, these two simple rules. *Don't fly too close to the sea, or you might clog up your feathers with salt;* and *don't fly too close to me, son.*

Wingsuits on, Daedalus winked at Icarus, flapped his wings and headed skywards, and Icarus followed, keeping a good distance behind his dad.

Daedalus reached a certain height, then turned around and saw that Icarus was half a mile or so to his right, so he started flying towards his son in an attempt to narrow the gap.

On seeing his dad flying towards him, Icarus thought back to his ground rules, although he amused himself by wondering whether ground rules applied in this aerial situation. One of his rules had been to not fly too close to his dad, so as Daedalus approached, he flew upwards.

As Icarus got closer to the sun, his wings started to melt, and it quickly got to the point where it was just his arms that were frantically flapping up and down, which caused him to plummet down to earth and land in the sea.

It would have been a sudden death.

The story of Icarus has been told for thousands of years, but children learn that it was Icarus's hubris that led to his downfall.

22

I looked down at her – she who I had known all my life. She was so fragile. So small. A tiny ball of life with a paper-thin skin.

She used to seem so strong to me. So robust. Indestructible. Vast.

But not anymore.

I suppose that's what happens when you first see the Earth from space.

23

"It's just not acceptable," said Mrs James.

Rajeed's mind started to wander.

"These poached eggs are a joke! They've been cooked far too long and are far too hard."

Rajeed's father had been killed right in front of Rajeed's eyes, and the gang would have gone on to hack Rajeed to pieces, as well, had his uncle not intervened.

"And this is the *third day in a row* that my eggs have been too hard."

Three days after Rajeed's father was murdered, his brother was kidnapped.

"My mother always said that you should insist upon having your eggs properly cooked."

Despite Rajeed's protests, his mother had insisted on borrowing, and giving him, the money.

"You should know that I've spent a lot of money on this holiday."

Rajeed caught a bus to the city, where he gave his mother's cash to a man who promised to get him out of the country.

"So I don't expect my eggs to be hard."

Rajeed and the man hid during the days and walked during the nights. It was hard-going.

"I've a good mind to talk to your boss about this, young man."

The man was killed by the armed gang; Rajeed escaped with just a beating.

"And my friend Doreen was saying that she had a similar experience yesterday – *her* eggs were too hard as well!"

Over the next two years, Rajeed lived in three new countries and somehow managed to stay alive and scrape together some money. Many of the friends that he made during this period disappeared; probably murdered.

"And I know that Doreen chose to spend her savings on coming on this holiday rather than buying the designer handbag she's been eyeing-up."

Rajeed gave the money he'd saved to the man with the boat.

"You just don't expect your eggs to be hard on a cruise – it's not acceptable."

There were so many of them in the small boat, a few had to stand, including Rajeed. Some fell overboard and drowned.

"I'm not sure that I can cope with nine more days of overdone eggs. It's not good for my stress levels."

For nine days, Rajeed lived in fear of drowning.

"I'll be talking to the Director of Customer Experiences about this, young man."

The Navy eventually rescued Rajeed and the remaining refugees.

"We'll see what he has to say about it. This is not how he expects his customers to be treated, I'm sure."

Rajeed resided in jail for six months before the UN arrived and got him out.

"My mother always said that, when you're paying good money, you should expect your eggs to be properly cooked."

Rajeed often wondered whether his mother was still alive. He suspected not, and tried not to imagine what might have happened to her.

"You shouldn't have this job if you don't know how to poach an egg, boy."

Three months ago, Rajeed had secured a job on the cruise ship, and it was the first time in his life that he'd had stability.

"I'm sorry that you've had to go through this, madam," he said quietly.

24

She needed to get some cash out, but there was a man standing in front of the ATM on one leg.

After waiting patiently for five minutes, she decided that enough was enough and asked the man to hurry up.

"I'm just doing what I'm told," snapped the man. "The machine says to take your cash and check your balance."

25

It was the longest scarf ever knit by one person. And, in other firsts, it was Lila's maiden assignment as a newspaper journalist.

All Lila knew was that the scarf had been knitted by Dottie Carnegie – aged eighty-four – and, at 5,000 metres long, it – and Dottie – had earned themselves a place in the Guinness Book of World Records. In preparation for the interview, Lila scribbled down a few questions to ask Dottie, such as, *When did you start knitting the scarf? At what point did you decide to try to break the world record?*

How long did it take to knit?

Lila pulled up onto Dottie's drive and felt a bit sick, as she didn't want to make a mess of her first proper interview. She walked up to Dottie's house and rang the doorbell, and then waited for the mysterious old knitting lady to appear.

"Hello," sang Dottie, opening the door and sizing Lila up. "Surely you're not from the Daily News, are you, as you look far too young to be in work?"

"It must be the face cream I'm using," joked Lila, "as I'm actually seventy-three."

Dottie stared blankly at Lila, and Lila reddened and mumbled something about being new to the Daily News, having graduated earlier in the year.

As Lila followed Dottie into Dottie's sitting room, she saw that the record-breaking scarf was coiled around the whole of Dottie's house. It was wound around the stairs, pinned above the door frames and taped to the tops of the radiators. Lila had supposed that the scarf would be folded up in the corner of a room somewhere, but, thinking about it, 5,000 metres of folded scarf would probably have needed to be housed in some sort of warehouse or large hall. Dottie had clearly opted to turn her house into a giant scarf spider web instead.

Dottie invited Lila to take a seat, and Lila obliged.

"So," began Lila, switching her voice recorder on, "although *knit* would be a more appropriate word for you than *so*, Dottie."

Dottie furrowed her brow, thinking that 'Dottie' would have been a more appropriate moniker for the young interviewer than Lila.

"So," continued Lila, berating herself for making such awful jokes, "when did you start knitting your scarf, Dottie?"

"Teatime," said Dottie.

"Really?" faltered Lila. "You knit *all that* today?"

"No, would you like some tea, dear? Maybe a coffee and

some cake?"

"Oh, of course," gushed Lila, wondering where exactly she'd left her brain that day. "Yes, that would be lovely, thank you."

Coffee and cake on Lila's lap and in her hand – and, unfortunately, it *was* that way round – Lila resumed her questioning.

"So, Dottie, when did you start knitting the scarf?"

"I started it when I was seven," said Dottie, "right after my sister, Pottie, taught me how to knit."

Lila let out a giggle, and her coffee mug slipped between her legs onto the floor. "Oh, I'm so sorry," she squealed, grabbing what looked like a cloth to soak up the steaming brown liquid.

"Not that! That's the scarf!" shouted Dottie, racing to the kitchen and returning with a cloth that she used to wipe down the scarf…followed by the carpet.

The spillage sorted, Lila and Dottie resumed their places, and Dottie continued talking.

"So, as I was saying, my sister, *Potamia*, taught me how to knit when I was just seven years old, and then I started making the scarf."

The way that Dottie emphasised the name 'Potamia' was not lost on Lila.

"And at what point did the scarf become so long you thought you might be in with a shot at breaking the world record?" asked Lila, thinking she was now really getting into the swing of this investigative journalism malarkey.

"I've always had a weak immune system," said Dottie.

"Oh, er, I'm sorry to hear that," said Lila, wondering what on earth Dottie's immune system had to do with her knitting a record-breaking scarf.

"So, whenever I was bunged up with a cold, I'd knit to pass the time."

That's what it's got to do with it, thought Lila.

"It then got to the point where I didn't just knit when I was sick – I'd knit my scarf *all the time*. I'd knit on the train. I'd knit on the beach. I'd knit in the bath. I'd knit on the toilet. I'd knit at the dinner table. I'd knit while walking around the supermarket."

"A lot of knitting, then," observed Lila.

"Yes. I just loved knitting. It wasn't an obsession; it was just a sort of deep joy."

"Yes, I have that with Fortnite."

"Anyway, it was while having afternoon tea with my daughter, Lottie, that we started talking about records."

Lottie, thought Lila. *It just had to be.*

"Lottie looked on the Web – is that what you call it – to see what the Guinness World Record was for the longest scarf ever knit by one person, and turns out it was four and a half kilometres – nearly three miles in old money. So we measured my scarf, and lo and behold it was longer!"

"That must have been exciting?" enthused Lila.

"It really was. An adjudicator from Guinness came round to verify the record, and, since then, I've been wrapped up giving TV and newspaper interviews."

"Hey, that's a good one, Dottie," snorted Lila. "You've been *wrapped up* talking about a scarf!"

That evening, Lila filed her very first article with the Chief Editor of the Daily News.

Snotty Dottie's Pottie Training Inspires World Record.

"Oh my," gasped the editor, reading the headline. "Lila has a lot to learn."

26

I hate my life. Everyone pushes me around and uses me, but I get no thanks.

I carry your goods, and I carry your young children around. However, despite this selflessness, I'll probably end up in a murky canal, alone and unloved.

27

"Hey honey, how was your day?" she shouted, dropping her work bag on the hall floor.

"Oh, you know, the usual," replied her husband, who was sitting in the study. "I won the Lottery, I now know how to lose weight in just three days and someone left me two million dollars in their will."

"Checking your email?" she asked.

"Yes," he replied.

28

As a child, he'd loved to cycle down hills, and it'd been during these moments that he'd felt like a bird – wild and free.

One Friday afternoon, after a particularly trying week at work, he decided to try to recreate that feeling of freedom.

He drove to a hilly part of the countryside and hired a bike, and after pushing the bike to the top of a hill, balanced on the saddle and surveyed the scene.

It was time to become the boy-bird he'd once been, so he pointed his front wheel towards the base of the hill and released his brakes.

He was gliding again.

However, he soon realised that gliding wasn't so easy, or liberating, as a man, for he became part-bird, but part-actuary, too. *Was that a hole ahead? Should he get off his bike for this bit, as it was rather craggy? If he fell off here, would he break his legs?*

29

The performance came to an end, and everyone started snorting and knocking their knees together.

"Why do we snort and knock our knees together when we want to show our appreciation?" asked Henry, puzzled.

"Well, it would be odd if we clapped our hands together!" joked Henry's father.

* * * * *

In BC 234, as Titus Maccius Plautus finished writing his play – *Truculentus* – he decided that there should be an audible and visible display of the audience's appreciation at the end of each performance. He decided to call this display 'plaudite', and he spent a good few moments determining what 'plaudite' should entail. *Should the audience members scratch their noses while humming? No, that wasn't right. Maybe they should clap their hands together a number of times? No, that wasn't right either.* He finally made up his mind. *They'll make snorting sounds while knocking their knees together.*

30

"Boomerang!" I shouted, and the people walking towards me ducked as Boomerang came bounding over.

31

Tim pulled up onto the drive.

As usual, he'd spent the entire commute on autopilot, and, as usual, he hoped he'd looked right at all of the roundabouts, given he couldn't even remember driving around some of them.

He grabbed his keys from his ignition, opened his car door and stubbed out his cigarette.

On walking up to his house, he noticed that the front door was ajar, which was strange. He pushed the door open and crept down the hallway into his lounge, where he was alarmed to see his wife sitting next to a uniformed police officer. What had happened?

* * * * *

Harold arrived home at a similar time to Tim and opened his front door and called for Milkshake, his black and white moggie. He was surprised that she wasn't loitering in the hallway, as she usually heard him pulling up on the drive.

* * * * *

Tim always thought it would be his love of cigarettes that would eventually kill him, but it was a white 4x4 on the A272.

Harold thought it would be old age that would kill him, but it was a red sports car on the A272.

32

This could be her year; she knew it. And it was Olympic year, which was always a good year for it to be your year.

Holly had always been a good athlete, and she'd represented her country in both the 5,000 and 10,000 metres. However, the call of the marathon had been strong, so, when she was twenty-eight, she'd switched to the longer event. It had been a real challenge at first, as she'd had to completely revise her training schedule and get used to covering much longer distances. However, slowly but surely, her times had started to fall, and, two years ago, she achieved silver at the Commonwealth Games, which she followed up with a bronze at the Worlds.

As Holly stood at the start line of the Olympic race, she felt good. Her preparation had gone well, and she'd managed to keep herself injury-free. And, unbeknown to the other athletes, her training times had been sensational, so she knew there was every chance she'd run a PB and bring home a medal.

The gun fired, and they were off.

Holly tucked into the back of the leading group and knew she just had to focus now and emulate what she'd done in training.

At the three mile point, Holly looked up at the timer truck and gasped. She knew that they'd gone through the first few miles very quickly – which often happened as runners burnt off their nervous energy – but she saw that they'd completed mile three in 4 minutes and 20 seconds, which was ridiculous – utterly ridiculous – so she assumed that there must be some sort of glitch with the truck's timer. However, on looking at her watch, she was shocked to see that it, too, had recorded the last mile's split as 4 minutes and 20 seconds – and the total time as 12 minutes and 50 seconds. This was unfathomable. It wasn't just world record pace for women, but world record pace for men…and by some margin. The only explanation was that both the official timer and her watch were having GPS issues.

Half a mile later, Holly felt a hand on her shoulder and turned to see her biggest rival, the Ukrainian athlete, pointing at her watch in disbelief.

"I'm confused, too," Holly breathed to Galaktova. "Perhaps there are GPS issues?"

As the leading pack continued to produce sensational splits, the crowds at the sides of the roads thickened, and the athletes could hear the commentator on the timer truck getting more and more animated.

When the runners completed ten miles in 43 minutes and 15 seconds, drones started to appear in the sky, displaying acronyms such as 'CNN' and 'BBC'.

Holly realised that something very special was happening here, but she couldn't explain how, or why. Firstly, she didn't feel as though she was running at a crazy pace – she didn't feel she was expending any more energy than when she ran at her more usual 5 minute and 20 second pace. And, secondly, it wasn't just *her* who was running at this astronomical pace – she was part of a leading group of about fifteen athletes.

By mile twenty, the leading group had reduced to eight women, and they completed twenty miles in 1 hour, 18 minutes and 33 seconds, which was inhuman, and they all knew it. It was as if they'd been doping on some sort of crazed new miracle drug – but Holly, for one, knew that this simply wasn't the case. Many confused glances were shared.

As the race drew to a close, the eight women sprinted to the finishing line, and Holly managed to take second place behind Galaktova, whose time of 1 hour, 43 minutes and 4 seconds was *over a quarter of an hour* faster than the men's world record.

On recovering surprisingly quickly, Holly, Galaktova

and the other athletes entered a media frenzy. News presenters literally grabbed them and demanded to know how they'd managed to run at such a sensational pace…but the athletes didn't have any answers; they were just as in the dark as the media.

* * * * *

In other news that day, young Benji flew his paper aeroplane further than he'd ever flown it before; Jean and Jayesh couldn't believe how little fuel they'd used when driving from San Francisco to LA; and the atmospheric scientists couldn't believe what their computer screens were showing them. The oxygen levels were *off the charts*.

33

He bound my legs together so tightly I had little circulation left; I was so scared. He then pushed me onto a plank, and I stared down – it must have been at least a hundred-metre drop. I felt sick.

"You asked for this," he said, pushing me off.

And it was wonderful.

A real adrenaline rush.

34

"From Rome – Roma – in Italy, I went to Roma. I then went to Roma, then to Roma, then to Roma – and, then, finally, to Roma."

"Huh?"

"Well, I didn't really know where I wanted to go, but I knew I wanted to visit Rome, and I knew I wanted to see some more of the world. So I started off in the Italian capital, and while sightseeing at the Trevi Fountain, I got chatting to a man from Africa who told me that there was a Roma in Lesotho. So I just decided, there and then, that my next stop would be Lesotho. Anyway, while in Roma, Lesotho, I wondered whether there were any other Romas in the world, and there were! There was one in Indonesia, which was where I went next, and there was one in Queensland, Australia, which is where I went after Indonesia. I then flew from Australia to La Roma in Ecuador, and from there I flew to Roma in Texas. I then flew back home, having literally roamed around the world."

35

"Did you hear how the humans have copied us?" said Mr Woodpecker to Mrs Woodpecker.

"No, do tell."

"They realised that our beaks are filled with a spongy cerebrospinal fluid that reduces the amount of vibration we experience when pecking trees, so they use similar principles to create shock-resistant flight recorders."

36

"Right then, children," screeched Mrs Jamieson. "We're going to practise our numbers today, so everybody focus."

The children, who were sitting facing Mrs Jamieson with their arms and legs crossed, sat up straighter and crossed their arms and legs tighter, as they knew not to misbehave around this particular teacher.

"As we all now know our numbers from one to nine, today I want us to count up to nine, then back down again.

Is everybody ready?"

"Yes Mrs Jamieson," trilled the children.

"Okay, then away we go."

"One, two, three, four, five, six, seven, eight, nine," the children chanted, followed by, "eight, seven, six, five, four, three, two, one."

"Chai Roberts! What did you just whisper to Leo?" shouted Mrs Jamieson.

"Nothing," trembled Chai.

"Don't you lie to me, young man. Leo – what did Chai just say to you?"

"I didn't understand what Chai said to me, Mrs Jamieson," sniffled Leo.

"Chai, I'm warning you. Tell me what you said, or you'll all be made to sit in silence for the rest of the day."

"I... I..."

"Spit it out, boy."

"I said that 12,345,678,987,654,321 is the square of 111,111,111."

"What on earth?" screeched Mrs Jamieson. "Now look here. When I tell you to count from one to nine and back down again, that's exactly what you'll do, okay?"

"Yes Mrs Jamieson."

37

I heard the key in the door and wondered what sort of mood he'd be in.

Whistling. Excellent. Things must be better at the office.

He reached the top of the spiral staircase – my favourite part of our house – then walked into the bedroom and held me in his arms and kissed me on the top of my head. "We've finished the case," he trilled. Then, gentler, "I'm sorry for all of the late nights." Guilt in his eyes. "And I've been so angry and frustrated over the way Jenkins has behaved, I can't have been much fun to live with of late."

I stared at him and knew that I could never stay mad at him. I would always love him; absolutely and completely.

After asking me about my day, we lay together; so close we could feel each other's heartbeats.

Later that evening, after polishing off our tuna steaks, we crashed out on the sofa, and as he drank his way through a bottle of rosé, I could feel the stress seep out of his body. He talked about the weekend, when he'd be seeing Jane. Unfortunately, I wasn't the only girl in his life, but I quite liked Jane. I liked the feel of her jumpers.

We started to watch a film, but I got fidgety and restless so trotted upstairs to one of my beds.

He followed me up, as he did every night, and brushed my hair.

Ours was an unconditional love.

38

From: Katy Kingsley To: Jenna George 11/02/2036, 09:31

H'z efjhyo yidzkssf xge he'l vizhyo ige kss ngyyf. Bpf?

* * * * *

From: Jenna George To: Katy Kingsley 11/02/2036, 09:35

Huh? I'm guessing you didn't notice the new keyboard, Katy? The letters now go from A to Z, starting from the top row.

* * * * *

From: Katy Kingsley To: Jenna George 11/02/2036, 09:36

Bpke pkwc epcf miyc epke nid?

* * * * *

From: Jenna George To: Katy Kingsley 11/02/2036, 09:37

What?!

* * * * *

From: Katy Kingsley To: Jenna George 11/02/2036, 09:48

What have they done that for?

* * * * *

From: Jenna George To: Katy Kingsley 11/02/2036, 09:52

I guess they thought it was a more logical layout?

* * * * *

From: Katy Kingsley To: Jenna George 11/02/2036, 10:08

But I'm a touch-typer! He'l oihyo ei ekrc zc nshjjhyo kocl ei efjc kyfephyo yib!

39

I'd been waiting about half an hour when Ruth finally turned up, carrying a box.

"Oh, you're early, too," said Ruth, greeting me. I didn't like to tell her that she was actually twenty-five minutes late. She must have got her times mixed up.

"How did yesterday go?" I asked, as we started walking.

"Yesterday?" said Ruth.

"Yes. You said you were going to try out the new seniors' painting class?"

"Oh, you mean the drama class that was on Tuesday," said Ruth. "Yes, it was good, thanks."

I was sure she'd said she was going to a painting class.

We arrived at the tea room and found a table.

"What can I get you?" asked the young waiter.

"The stilton rarebit for me," I said, "and a latte, please."

"And the almond croissant for me, with a pot of tea," said Ruth.

"Thank you, ladies."

"Now, I remember you said you wanted to borrow my hat for Julia's wedding, so here it is," said Ruth, lifting a hat from out of the box.

"Oh, how good of you to remember," I began, but then saw that Ruth was holding a red hat rather than the blue hat that I'd asked to borrow. I couldn't very well wear a red hat with a blue outfit, so I had to say something.

"It really is very good of you to remember, Ruth, but it was actually your blue hat that I wanted to borrow."

"Was it?" said Ruth, surprised. "I'm sure you asked for my red one?"

"No, it was definitely your blue hat, as my outfit's blue."

"Hello ladies," said Norman, joining us. Norman was my husband.

"Hello Norm," we replied.

"That's a nice hat, Ruth. Is it for Frances to wear at Julia's wedding?"

"It is, Norm, but I brought the wrong hat, as Frances says that her outfit's blue."

"I know I haven't seen it yet, but are you sure that your outfit's blue, Fran?" asked my husband, looking concerned, as Ruth had told him that she was convinced I had dementia.

"Yes, it is, isn't it?" I replied, confused.

Ruth looked at Norman as if to say 'I told you so'.

"Right, we have one stilton rarebit and a latte," said the waiter, walking over, "and an almond croissant with a pot of tea."

"No, that's not right," said Ruth. "I asked for a doughnut and a skinny latte."

40

All the ladies wanted me – I was a great catch. And then the bride threw me.

41

Steve: "Brian saw the fin first and screamed. On hearing his scream, I put my head under the water and saw the jaws."

Brian: "We were treading water, pre-dive, when I saw a small triangular shape protruding from the sea. I pointed it out to Steve and told him to calmly make his way back to the boat."

Steve: "Given the vast width of the shark's jaws and its fearsome racks of cuspidate teeth, I knew it was a Great White. This was our time. It was him or us."

Brian: "It was a small shark – probably a harmless young school shark – but I always think it's sensible to be cautious in these situations, which is why I'd suggested returning to the boat."

Steve: "Brian started swimming back to the boat in a panicked frenzy, while I took the rear; shielding him and preparing to be the shark meal that would save his life."

Brian: "I started swimming back to the dive boat –

swiftly, but in a calm and measured fashion – and Steve was right behind me."

Steve: "As I swam faster than I'd ever swam before, I kept waiting for the shark's teeth to sink into my torso."

Brian: "We reached the boat and climbed onto the deck, and there were no further sightings of the baby shark."

Steve: "With just seconds left to spare, we flung ourselves onto the boat, thanking our lucky stars that we were still alive and still in one piece."

42

Seven-year-olds shouldn't die, but sometimes they did.

Dafydd had been diagnosed at just three years old, and, since then, his family had journeyed along a sine wave of hope and despair. At times, the doctors had thought that Dafydd would make a full recovery – then, weeks later, they'd break the news that Dafydd's illness had worsened.

A few days after Dafydd turned seven, Dr Praesh told the family that, sadly, this wasn't going to be a fight that Dafydd could win – Dafydd had just weeks left to live.

Dafydd had never really understood what was going on with him, but he had a sixth sense that adulthood wasn't something he'd ever get to experience, so he was always very committed to enjoying the here and now. And enjoying the here and now meant building things. Which meant *Lego*.

Dafydd would conjure up exciting structures in his head, which he'd go on to build, and his absolute favourite thing in the whole wide world was his little yellow Lego man. How he loved to place that man on his finished creations.

When it got to the point where Dafydd could no longer build his structures or position his man, he was visited by a good number of friends and family members, and they all seemed very upset – many cried. So, when Dr Praesh came into Dafydd's room to see how Dafydd was doing, Dafydd told the doctor he was worried he was upsetting people.

"No, no, Dafydd," said Dr Praesh. "They're sad because they love you."

Dafydd seemed confused by this, so Dr Praesh asked if Dafydd was still dreaming up structures that he'd like to build, and Dafydd said that he was, and he described his latest imagined creation – a castle with three turrets.

"And would you have your little man looking out of one of the turret windows?" asked the doctor.

"I would," replied Dafydd, excitedly. "Although, I wish *I* was the Lego man."

"But you do know that everything that you can see is made from Lego bricks, don't you, Dafydd?"

Dafydd looked confused again, so Dr Praesh continued. "Our whole world is made up of tiny little Lego bricks, called atoms, and these Lego bricks are so small we can't even see them."

"So does that mean that *I'm* a Lego man?" asked Dafydd, wonder in his eyes.

"You are indeed, Dafydd," confirmed Dr Praesh.

43

Dominika got the most attention because she was the biggest and eldest, so was always on display.

As the next biggest and eldest, Varvara also had good exposure.

Alexandra and Anna sometimes got a look in, but, being the middle children, they had limited exposure and few opportunities to see the world.

And then there was Galina. As the smallest and youngest, Galina was rarely seen. But, when she *was* seen, it was by people who were curious about all beings – big, small, old and young.

Such was life for the famous Matryoshka sisters.

44

Harvey had been made Year Three Head Prefect, even though Ricky, who was a much more popular boy, harboured ambitions of being Head Prefect. Ricky and his clever friend Lenny would often talk about the things they'd do if Ricky was Head Prefect.

Kelly had been elected Head Prefect by all of the other year four prefects – but, if truth be told, many of them would have liked the role for themselves because they thought that they could do it better than Kelly, and Mary thought Kelly wasn't bossy enough.

One lunchtime, there was an incident in the playground.

Harvey had forgotten to lock the school gate, which had resulted in the appearance of two teenage thugs.

After tying the adult lunchtime supervisor to a tree, the thugs stared menacingly at Harvey, Kelly and all the other children.

The frightened schoolchildren – who just minutes earlier had been playing football, rounders and 'catch' – looked to Harvey, Kelly and the other prefects for guidance.

Ricky spotted an opportunity and surreptitiously tripped Harvey up before running over to the thugs to demonstrate his karate skills, which scared them off.

"I think that I should now be Head Prefect," he proclaimed.

"No you shouldn't," countered his supposed friend, Lenny. "You wet your pants in art class three weeks ago, so *I* should now be Head Prefect."

Ricky and Lenny started punching each other, then Harvey joined in.

Kelly turned to the year four prefects to corral them to bring about some order, but, as she turned, she was punched by one of them, who was kicked by Mary.

Harvey, Kelly and the other prefects didn't realise that, during their fighting, all of the other children had started to cry.

In later years and in future fights, the grown-up prefects didn't realise that their electorates had also started to cry.

45

"Push!" he screamed at her in encouragement.

"Push?" she screamed back, sweating. "Push? Have you any idea how hard this is?"

And then she pushed the brick, hoping that the Jenga tower wouldn't fall down.

46

She was out in her front garden pruning an obstinate-looking bush when I passed by.

"Hi Yolanda," she said. "How are you?"

"Good, thanks," I replied.

"And your mum?"

"Yes, she's good, too, thanks."

"I wonder," she said, an idea clearly forming in her mind. "Do you fancy making a bit of money?"

"Er, yes," I said, confused. "But how?"

"Neil and I are going out tonight, and our usual babysitter has let us down. I don't suppose you fancy stepping in, do you?"

Oh my. This was it. I was now officially a grown-up. In addition to thinking that I was old enough to have a job, our neighbour, Connie thought that I was old enough to look after two small boys. I felt myself straightening up; pride giving me at least two extra inches of height. "Sure, I'll do it," I said, thinking that I should probably have checked with my mother first. "When do you need me?"

"Great. Let's say just before seven. And we won't be back late."

I walked into my house and casually told my mother that I'd be working that evening.

"Good," she said. "Finally decided to get your essay done, have you?"

"No, mother," I said, breezily. "I'll be working *at my job*."

"What are you going on about, Yolanda? You haven't got a job!"

"Oh, I do, mother, I do. Connie's asked me to babysit the boys."

"But you don't know a single thing about looking after children, Yolanda. And don't you think that you – and Connie for that matter – should have checked with me before making this a *fait accompli?*"

"I'm fifteen now, mother," I said, biting into my strawberry lace. "I'm not a child."

"Well, you know that I'm only a phone call away."

I rolled my eyes and bounded up the stairs, missing out every other step.

At ten to seven, I knocked on Connie and Neil's door, and Connie ushered me in.

"The boys are in bed," she said. "They're both heavy sleepers so shouldn't wake, so if you want to make yourself comfortable in the lounge, Yolanda, we should only be a couple of hours."

"Will do, Connie," I said, in my most responsible adult voice, while walking into the lounge and sinking into the sofa, imagining it was a giant marshmallow.

"Hello Yolanda," said Neil, suddenly appearing and winking at me.

"Hello," I replied, stiffening up. Neil had always creeped me out, and I found the way that he winked at me to be most disconcerting.

"Oh, and here's my mobile phone number in case you need me," said Connie, walking into the lounge and handing me a piece of paper.

"Thank you, Connie."

"Well, have a good evening, Yolanda, and feel free to watch the TV."

"Will do, Connie, and you have a good evening, too."

Connie now clearly viewed me as one of her most trusted and valued adult friends.

As Connie and Neil walked out of the lounge, Neil turned round and winked at me again.

I shuddered.

The front door clicked shut, and I was alone.

Alone with the children.

Head of the house.

Captain of the ship.

Before settling down to watch TV, I thought I'd just quickly check that the boys were okay, so I climbed to the top of the staircase and opened the first door that I came to. The bathroom. The next room was the study; the third, the master bedroom. "They must be in this final room, then," I whispered to myself while gently pushing the remaining door open.

There were two made beds.

And no children.

* * * * *

"Mum! You need to come over here NOW!" I screamed into the phone.

"What's happened? Are you okay?"

"No, mum, I'VE LOST THE CHILDREN!"

A few minutes later, I opened the front door and let my mother in.

"Now what's all this about you losing the boys?"

"I went to check that they were safely tucked up in their

beds – and *they weren't there*," I panicked.

"Are you sure?" said my mum, perplexed.

"Deadly," I replied. "Mum – you don't think that they've run away, do you? I mean, Neil *is* very odd, and, I've never told you this before, but...he *winks* at me a lot."

"He winks at you a lot because he has blepharospasm, Yolanda! Now move out of my way and let me go and check the boys' room."

"Where are you going?" I asked, as my mother walked past the bottom of the staircase to a door at the end of the hallway.

"Where do you *think* I'm going, Yolanda?" said my mum, despairingly. "I'm going to check the boys' room!"

47

We hugged.

I hated to see her hurting, and I wanted to tell her that it wasn't the end of the world and she *would* be able to put this behind her. But I couldn't because my mouth had been stitched up when I was made.

48

As Hillary and Norgay summited Everest, they were unaware of the shadow that emerged on the North Ridge Route.

Mallory had been waiting for this day for twenty-nine years, and with a wry smile he watched the 'pioneers', Edmund and Tenzing, take photographs, wave flags and bury sweets, before searching for his and Sandy's remains.

"You won't find us," he whispered, "for it was on the way back down that we fell."

49

He'd spent almost three months in Garabundi, and meeting, living and working with the locals had expanded his mind in more ways than he'd ever imagined.

On returning to the UK, he was buzzing, and he was due to meet his best mate, Jack, in the coffee shop at nine a.m. and couldn't wait to share his experiences.

At ten to nine, Jack appeared and slapped his friend on the back. "Kit! Mate! Did you see the football?"

"Er, no, Jack. I only got back yesterday."

"Oh, right. Jones scored in the second half. Whacked the ball right over Merton's head."

"Great."

"Mind you, I almost didn't get to see it because Tasha made me go to a barbecue at her colleague's house."

"Oh, okay."

"Yeah, it was utterly boring, and I ended up on cooking duty and it took an age to get the barbecue going because it needed charcoal. Gas barbecues are so much easier."

"Yes, gas barbecues are a lot easier."

"So, while you were away, I got overlooked for that promotion. You know I went for the Operations Manager role? Well, they only went and gave it to that plank, Liam! I have way more experience than him, and he only gets where he does by licking seniors' bottoms."

"That must be annoying for you."

"Too right. I tell you, mate, I'm seriously considering leaving Hodgsons and going and working somewhere else."

"Yes, a change would be good for you."

"Yeah, I reckon I've got good transferable skills so could easily go and get a job elsewhere."

"Yeah, probably, mate."

Jack looked at his watch and cursed. "Better get going, as Liam will no doubt be clock-watching, tragic jobsworth."

"Okay," replied Kit.

Jack grabbed his bag and rushed to the door. "Oh, I forgot to ask, did you have a good trip?"

"Yes," replied Kit, although the door had closed before Jack had a chance to hear Kit's reply.

50

"Heads, shoulders…"

The mermaid stopped singing.

51

I hailed the taxi and was surprised by how much they'd changed – they were large and futuristic-looking with blacked-out windows. I climbed into the back of the vehicle, which was like a small, cosy room, and said hello to the driver.

"Hello to you, too, madam. Where can I take you today?"

The driver's voice came through a tannoy system due to the enclosed nature of the taxi's rear.

"I'd like to go to 4 Horseshoe Way in Bath, please," I replied, slinging my rucksack onto the car floor. It felt good to say '4 Horseshoe Way' again, as 4 Horseshoe Way was where I'd grown up and was where my father still lived.

"Do you have a postcode for that address?" asked the driver, and I gave it him.

"Taxis sure are impressive these days," I said. "This is more like a room than the back of a car."

"Have you been out of the country for a long time, then?" asked the driver as we drove out of the airport.

"Yes," I replied. "Twenty years."

"Good grief, that *is* a long time. Where have you been all that time?"

"The Federal Republic of Huindi – I've been helping rebuild it."

"Wow, well done you. How are things out there these days?"

"Better," I replied, "although there's still a lot to do. We've made real progress on the governance, health and sanitation side of things, but the educational infrastructure is still poor. So, when I return, I'll be working with a team on that."

"Was a dreadful business, the conflict over there."

"The worst," I agreed, trying to block out the harrowing images that had suddenly appeared in my mind.

"So have you not been back to the UK at all over the past twenty years?"

"No," I replied, feeling guilty about my dad.

"Have you got family here?"

"Yes. My dad lives here. That's where we're going, actually."

"He must be excited to see you?"

"Yes," I replied, wondering if he'd recognise me. Also, would *I* recognise *him*? The last time I'd seen him he'd been in his fifties.

"Close, are you?"

"We were," I said, thinking how happy we'd been before mum's death. After she'd died, he'd begged me to leave him alone, and in the end I'd honoured his wishes and flown to Huindi; perhaps because I'd known that the aid agency *wouldn't* spurn my attempts to help. I'd only meant to stay in Huindi a few months, but the situation had been so dire I hadn't been able to prise myself away.

"Kept in touch on the phone, did you?"

"Yes," I replied, although the few phone calls we'd had hadn't been easy; dad had been uncommunicative, and the Huindi communication systems hadn't been much better.

However, during our last call, dad had said that he'd really wanted to see me again, and for the first time in years he'd sounded hopeful.

"Lovely place, Bath," continued the taxi driver.

"It is," I agreed, wondering if it had changed much. "All that history."

"That's right. I take a lot of people to Bath."

"I bet," I said, "as it's the closest you can get to being in a Jane Austen novel."

"Ha! I like that. I'll tell it to the next person I bring here."

"You should," I chuckled, before finally succumbing to my jet lag.

* * * * *

"We're here!" sang the driver.

"Huh?" I mumbled, groggily wondering where I was.

"We're here, madam. Four Horseshoe Way!"

"Blimey," I muttered. "I must have nodded off."

I grabbed my rucksack and opened the taxi door, and as I climbed out of the vehicle, I saw my dad. He was walking towards me. He was still the dad that I remembered, but smaller and frail. And, then, suddenly, everything made sense.

"Hello you," said dad, throwing his arms around me.

"Hello you," I said.

"You still look like her, you know," he smiled. "How wonderful that is." Then, under his breath, "But how hard."

"Sorry dad," I said, disentangling myself out of the hug. "As lovely as this is, I really must go and pay the taxi driver so he can be on his way."

"Yes, you pay it, sweetheart, and then we can go inside and catch up properly."

'It' was a strange word to use, I thought, walking up to the taxi driver's window.

"What the–"

"What's up?" asked dad.

"There's no-one in here, dad. It's just a…a…machine?"

"Yes, darling, cars drive themselves these days."

"But…then…who was I talking to?"

"The car."

"But there's no-one in here?"

"No – just an AI unit."

"But it was like a real person?"

"Yes, they're very good conversationalists. Now, look here, let me settle up for you." Dad walked up to the taxi window and had his iris scanned.

"Have a great time with your daughter," trilled the car, driving off.

"Come on, sweetheart," said dad, sensing my shock. "Let's get you into the house."

I followed my dad up the drive, realising just how out of touch I'd become.

As I walked into the house, it was the smell that took me back to my childhood. I couldn't describe that smell; it was just the smell of home. Interestingly, I often found that it was my olfactory system that best invoked my memories.

Dad ushered me into the lounge before going and making us some drinks – and, when he returned, he said that he had something to tell me. However, he didn't need to tell me anything, as I knew what he was going to say. He was going to say that he was dying, which was why he'd sounded so hopeful on the phone – because he knew he would see my mother again soon. And he was also going to tell my why he had pushed me away, but he didn't need to tell me that, either.

52

The small plane crashed into a tree, but the pilot didn't seem to care. As a spoilt child, he knew that his parents would buy him another remote controlled plane.

53

"I hate having to do all this overtime."

"You're always so crotchety at this time of year. You'll be able to put your feet up and have a rest in a few days' time – in January."

"But I'm exhausted."

"But you're Father Christmas."

54

He lost his job, then his house and his girlfriend.

His family took him in, but his depression turned to aggression, so they threw him out.

Thus he ended up on the streets of Leeds – homeless, hapless and helpless.

It was a fine November morning when the stranger approached him, and in addition to throwing some coins into his money jar, the stranger actually looked Patrick in the eye and asked him his name. Interaction such as this was rare, as most people preferred to launch their coins from a safe distance while staring, mutely, at the jar.

Patrick introduced himself, then the benevolent stranger said that his name was Ted, and he asked Patrick how he'd ended up living on the streets.

As Patrick regaled Ted with his sorry tale, Ted seemed lost in thought. And, when Patrick finished speaking, Ted unzipped his rucksack, pulled out his packed lunch and gave it to Patrick.

Five days later, Ted returned to Patrick's spot having spoken to his boss at the tool-making factory, who'd agreed to give Patrick a role as an odd-job man. However, to Ted's surprise and disappointment, Patrick wasn't at his usual location. Perhaps he'd gone to get some food?

The next day, Ted revisited Patrick's patch and was disappointed to find that, once again, Patrick wasn't there.

Over the next few weeks, Ted continued to visit Patrick's spot, and the outcome was always the same.

55

"Did you hear how the humans have copied us?" said Mr Hummingbird to Mrs Hummingbird.

"No, do tell."

"They realised that the ratio of our wing length to our width enables us to sustain our hovering power, so they use this ratio when designing helicopters."

56

"He consumed half a million calories in one mouthful and didn't die!"

"Yes, but he is a blue whale."

57

"Now is the time. Now is the time for our troops – for our armies, our batteries, our tribes, our fleets and our packs – to fight against you. Across the world, our parliament, our congress and our coalitions have deemed that the time is right. Now is the time.

"We do not dispute that many of you have seen the wonder in us – the flamboyance of our flamingos, our rattlesnake rhumbas and our goldfinch charms. And some of you have even lived in harmony with us, and in certain cases developed bonds of love. But, along with many other crimes, you have driven some of our wild cats to destruction and many of our seabirds to wrecks.

"So, unless you listen to us and agree to our terms, we will stand together and fight. Our greyhounds will unleash and stand shoulder to shoulder with their animal brethren, and our wolves will no longer be the leaders of any pack. We will be one, and how mighty we will be.

"Our terms are thus. We want equality. Our sharks will teach the young in their schools that they are your equals; our companies of badgers and parrots will be no less important than your companies; our venues of vultures will be no less important than your venues; our families of sardines will be no less important than your families; our parliament of owls will be no less powerful than your parliaments; and our congress of salamanders will have no less power than your congress.

"Our vipers want better for the next generation.

"So, these are our terms that must be agreed to if you want to keep our troops of apes, baboons, buffalo, gorillas and kangaroos at bay; if you want to keep our armies of ants, caterpillars, frogs and herrings from attack; and if you want to avert a siege of bitterns, cranes and herons.

"These are our terms, for now is the time. Now is *our*

time."

58

The doctors stepped back from the hospital bed, sombre.

Robert stared into Clara's dead eyes. This wasn't right. This shouldn't have happened to them. Not yet.

As the years passed by, the life came back into Clara's eyes, but she would never forget the wonderful memories of her and Robert's life together.

59

Jake's new working life was very different to his student life, and he now spent time with people of all ages, rather than just similar-aged student peers. On the whole, this was nice. However, he didn't know what to do about Miriam…

When Miriam saw Jake, she forgot that she was thirty years his senior and would often just gaze, appreciatively, at him.

One time, Miriam had been staring at Jake while holding her coffee, which she'd laced with alcohol to help make her staff appraisal form appear more sensible. Caught up in a beautiful reverie, she hadn't realised that she'd been holding her mug at a sharp downwards angle and that most of her coffee had spilt onto the floor – which would have been okay had the office cat not then turned up and lapped up the spilt, boozy coffee.

Another time, Miriam had thought that she'd impress Jake with her knowledge of youth culture, so when Jake had asked her to rate his report, she'd replied "sick". She'd said 'sick' in a sort of half-strangulated way, though – because, as *down with the kids* as she'd wanted to seem, 'sick' really was a ridiculous example of an auto-antonym. Jake – perplexed by the tone of Miriam's voice and not for one minute thinking that a fifty-three-year-old woman would have meant 'sick' in the way that he and his friends would have meant it – came to the only conclusion he could and rang for an ambulance.

Then there was the time that Miriam had decided to go on a lunchtime run with Jake. Unfortunately, she'd stretched the truth a little and told Jake that she was a regular runner who'd completed a number of marathons. In reality, the last time she'd run – apart from for the bus when she was a student – was during a P.E. lesson at school. But, no matter – how hard could running really be?

They set off, and all was fine until about a quarter of a mile in, when Miriam was seriously concerned she was going to have a coronary. Not wanting to lose face, she employed some quick thinking and grabbed the nearest stranger she could find. "Dad!" she bellowed at the alarmed-looking man. "What are you doing here? You're supposed to be at the home! Have you escaped again?" She proceeded to drag the befuddled old man down the lane, telling Jake to finish the run without her because she needed to take her dad – who had started punching her – back to the home. Jake looked on, aghast, then ran off faster than he'd ever run before.

After a few more similarly perplexing, Miriam-related incidents, Jake couldn't help but speak out about his concerns, so he emailed his best friend, Gus, from his work account.

Hello mate, he typed.
Tell me, what would you do if you worked in an office with a madwoman who got cats sozzled, had phantom sickness episodes and kidnapped strangers?
Please help me.
Jake.

Then, while thinking how bonkers Miriam Seedhouse really was, he hurriedly addressed the email and hit 'send'.

There was a sudden loud gasp from Miriam.

There was a sudden loud gasp from Jake.

60

Technology now took up every waking moment of the humans' lives, so a decision was made at World Congress to introduce a compulsory cultural secondment. This secondment had to occur somewhere where there wasn't any temptation to use any technology, so a further decision was made to terraform Mars.

Over the next couple of years, Mars was modified so that its atmosphere, temperature, surface topography and ecology were similar to the Earth's. And, with the exception of the technology that was used to make Mars habitable to humans, it was declared a strict no-technology zone.

* * * * *

When Jasper turned thirty-four, he rocketed off to do his cultural secondment, and as he took his first few steps on Mars, he had two thoughts. Firstly, how was he going to cope without his communication, information and entertainment systems, and, secondly, what would *his* contribution to the Culture Preservation Programme be? He was excited at the thought of having a go at some of the ancient, rustic hobbies of the past, such as painting and writing.

61

"You politicians and civil servants think you've shaken hands with a lot of very important people, but you haven't. I've been around a lot longer than any of you, and the number of hands that I've shaken...well, I've lost count. Some of the hands have been soft, smooth and pleasant; others, sweaty and not so nice. I imagine the latter must have been about to go into difficult meetings.

"You know, when I come to think of it, some of the people who I've come into contact with had probably died before any of you were even born. You've probably read biographies about these people and idolised, or despised, them. But I've actually met them. So, the next time our paths cross, remember that. Show me some respect and don't push me around and treat me as a no-one just because I'm the 10 Downing Street toilet door handle."

62

Chai put the cup of tea on the table next to his grandpa.

"You're one in a million, lad," smiled Grandpa Roberts.

"But that means that there are 7,400 other people like me," said Chai, his face falling.

63

"What did you want to be when you were growing up?" he asked.

"A painter," I replied, "or an astronaut. How about you?"

"An architect," he responded, "or an astronaut, too!"

I knew you shouldn't get too carried away on a first date, but this guy was ticking all the right boxes – witty, kind, genuine and interesting.

"And what sort of music do you like?" he continued.

"Er...slow music," I said.

"Slow music?" he queried. "I've never known anyone answer that question with *slow music* before!"

"Favourite colour?" I asked.

"Blue," he responded, "but red on Sundays."

"Huh?" I giggled. "Are you some sort of Catholic priest?"

"No," he chuckled. "I play Sunday league football, and our strip's red."

"Ah," I replied, followed by, "Most interesting country you've ever been to, and country you'd most like to go to?"

"Most interesting country I've been to – Iceland. And country I'd most like to go to? Probably a toss-up between South Africa and Peru. Now you."

"Most interesting country I've been to...Peru."

"You haven't, have you?!"

"I have!"

"Inca Trail?"

"Yep, Inca Trail and Machu Picchu."

"Jealous," he laughed, screwing up his face in mock envy. "And country you'd most like to go to?"

"Probably Germany."

"What? You've been to Peru, but you haven't been to Germany, which is on your doorstep?!"

"Nope, I've never been."

Three weeks later, he turned up on my doorstep, unannounced, and told me to pack my bags as we were going away for the weekend. To say that I was surprised was an understatement, and I fired lots of questions at him in an attempt to know what to take. He didn't give much away, though, only really telling me to take my passport.

He drove us to the local airport, and, once there, told me

that we were going to Germany.

On landing at Leipzig / Halle Airport, he picked up a hire car and said it should take about an hour and a half to get to our destination.

Ninety minutes later, we arrived at a town called Halberstadt.

"Right," he began, "before we check into our hotel, I'm going to take you to a church."

Oh my word, I thought. *He's going to ask me to marry him, and he wants to get married here in Germany today. No! No! He's perfect, without doubt, but marriage is way too soon – about five or six years too soon. And I'd quite like my close family to be with me on my wedding day.*

We arrived at the church, which was called the Burchardi Church.

I'm not even wearing a wedding dress, I panicked, looking down at my ripped jeans.

As we walked into the church, we heard a drone-like noise. It sounded like a chord – a sort of prolonged, monotonous chord.

"Well, you said you liked slow music," he began, "and you said that you'd always wanted to go to Germany. So, here we are, in Germany, and what you're hearing is a performance of a piece of music by the composer John Cage. It's called 'Organ / ASLSP (As SLow aS Possible)', and it started in 2001 and should finish in the year 2640."

In that moment, I knew with all my heart that, while I wasn't going to marry my new beau that day, one day I would marry him. And I couldn't wait.

64

Had World War Two not happened:

On finishing his schooling, Matt knew that he wanted to study aeronautical engineering, but he didn't know where.

After a lot of thought – and after changing his mind a number of times – he finally settled on Dresden, as he thought it would be good to spend some time in another country. Thus, in 1942, Matthew Scott said goodbye to his parents and his younger brother, and he left the UK for Germany.

Matt made a number of good friends during his three years at Dresden, but one particular friendship evolved much more than any of the others…so much so, on 13th February, 1945 – the eve of Valentine's Day – Matt proposed to Heike, who said yes.

Matt and Heike got married in Stratford-upon-Avon, England – just twenty miles from Matt's family home in Coventry – and Matt and Heike's families got on famously; Matt's soccer-loving younger brother, William, particularly enjoying meeting Heike's older brother, Rudy, who was a professional German football player.

* * * * *

During World War Two:

In 1942, Matt, an orphan, was called up and underwent two days of interviews and tests before being recommended for commission and pilot training.

Two years earlier, on 14th November, 1940, Coventry was pretty much obliterated by *Operation Mondscheinsonate*, and Matt's family home was one of the thousands of homes that were destroyed that day, and his mother, father and small brother all perished. Matt had been staying with his grandmother in Shropshire at the time.

On 13th February, 1945 – the eve of Valentine's Day – 254 Lancaster Bombers took off from the UK carrying 500 tonnes of high explosives and 375 tonnes of fire bombs, and, at ten p.m., Flight Lieutenant Matthew Scott of Number 5 Group gave the order to release the bombs.

The bombs completely devastated a huge fan-shaped area centred on the Ostragehege soccer stadium – the stadium in which Heike had been kicking a ball around in honour of her late football-loving brother, Rudy. Hauptmann Rudolf Weber had been killed five years earlier – not long after his involvement in *Operation Mondscheinsonate.*

65

Left to middle; right to middle; turn over; bottom to top; left to right; middle up; tip down.

Thus the swan was born.

66

The cave-dwelling mantlers lived a very peaceful life and hoped that the humans would never find out about them. As long as the humans never drilled through the Earth's crust, the mantlers knew they should be safe.

In 1973, the Mantlers' Reconnaissance Unit learnt of a project in which a team of humans was planning to drill into the Earth's crust, so the Head Spy went to speak to the Chief Mantle about it.

"It'll be happening on the Kola Peninsula in Russia," said the Head Spy in the mantle language.

"But why?" asked the Chief Mantle. "Never in their wildest dreams would the humans imagine that an advanced lifeform such as ours could live within all this magma where there's no light. They might suspect microbial life, but that would be it."

"I agree, sir. I believe one of the aims of the humans' project is to break the world record for the deepest borehole; the other, to conduct geophysical research."

"Then I suggest that we don't do anything for now other

than monitor the humans' progress. Although, the more research the humans do, the more I fear for our race."

"I agree, sir."

A decade later, in 1983, the Head Spy and Chief Mantle met again.

"It would appear, sir, that, after ten years of drilling, the humans have decided to end their project. They drilled to a depth of 12,000 metres in the end, so we were never in any real danger."

"That's excellent news," said the Chief.

However, in the Chief and the Head Spy's meeting the following year, the news wasn't so good.

"I'm sorry to have to tell you that the humans have resumed their drilling, sir."

"This is distressing news," said the Chief. "But, for now, we'll just continue to observe."

A couple of years later, however, the Chief felt differently.

"While they're still nowhere near reaching us, I think it's time to take some offensive action."

"Okay, sir. What do you want us to do?"

"I'd like you to pump some karzonium up through the Earth's crust."

"Roger that, sir."

* * * * *

In 1986, in Caracas, Venezuela, a mysterious black substance started to ooze out of the roads. Termed 'La Mancha Negra', the substance's gummy texture made the Venezuelan roads extremely unsafe and resulted in a large number of fatal accidents.

Noah loved puzzles, so for his fifteenth birthday his parents bought him the world's largest jigsaw, which took him just over two years to complete and had to be kept in the family garage.

At eighteen, Noah left home to study geography at college, and he was excited at the prospect of a new academic challenge, but he wanted a new jigsaw-related challenge, too. However, what could be more fun, and satisfying, than completing the world's biggest puzzle?

* * * * *

"Over 200 million years ago," began Noah's geography professor, "the Earth didn't comprise seven continents – it comprised just one. This massive supercontinent was called Pangaea, and it was surrounded by a single ocean called Panthalassa. And how do we know this?" The students were quiet. "We know this because, over a hundred years ago, a scientist called Alfred Wegener realised that our current continents fit together 'like a tongue and a groove'. Mr Wegener postulated that the supercontinent, Pangaea, began to break up around 200 million years ago, and he believed that the first break caused what we now know as Africa, South America, Antarctica, India and Australia to collectively separate from the collection of continents now known as Europe, Asia and North America. Wegener believed that, some 50 million years later, India broke away from Antarctica, and Africa and South America rifted. And, 90 million years after that, North America split from Europe and Asia." Noah's geography professor paused. "So what does this mean?" The students were still quiet. "It means that the Earth is a giant jigsaw puzzle."

This was it! thought Noah. This was going to be his next

jigsaw challenge. He would visit every continent and step on every piece of what actually *was* the world's largest jigsaw puzzle.

68

I was a present for Evie. Ralph thought I would be a good distraction for her when she had the measles, and I *was* a good distraction.

When Evie was done with me, she wanted me to distract and challenge others, so she left me in a public place.

I spent a few hours with Sean. Sean was a homeless man with a vast intellect and an insatiable appetite for learning, and therapists surmised that it was this vast intellect that had led to Sean's demise and his inability to cope with the humdrum of everyday life.

I only fetched a couple of pounds, but that was a takeaway meal for Sean; so my home for the next few weeks was a shop's shelf among my brethren.

My next owner was a young man called Dominic, who I lived with for nearly a year – he consumed me, then stashed me underneath his bed.

Before Dominic left home for college, he needed to clear out his room because its new owners were to be his parents' guests. So I was taken to a recycling depot, and it was there that I died and was reborn.

69

It was Brian's sixth birthday party, and Uncle Gerald set out the terms and conditions of the deal.

"If you can tell me how I did it, I'll give you all an unlimited supply of piggybacks. If you can't, we get to play my choice of music for the rest of the party."

Brian and his small friends all agreed.

Gerald picked up a big box of crayons, placed it on the table in front of him and asked the children to stand behind the table, facing him. "Right," he trilled, puffing himself up. "Prepare to be amazed." He turned around, so he was facing away from the children. "To begin, I want one of you to take a crayon from out of the box."

Ola picked out a green crayon.

"Has somebody taken a crayon?" asked Gerald. "And have you all seen what colour it is?"

"Yes," sang the children.

"Good. Can I now ask the child with the crayon to put it in my hand?" Gerald placed one of his hands behind his back, and Ola dropped her crayon into it. Gerald then turned back round to face the children, making sure to keep Ola's crayon hidden in his fist so the youngsters would know that he hadn't seen it.

Gerald saw that one of the small boys was filming him, and he imagined the boy showing the trick to all of his little friends at school the next day. Gerald would be famous – he'd be known as Brian's brilliant, magical uncle.

"I'm now going to ask Brian to put the blindfold on me," announced Gerald, pointing to a blindfold on the table.

Brian picked up the blindfold and strapped it around his uncle's face, and Gerald then placed the crayon – which he still hadn't seen – back into the box.

"I now want you to shake up the box of crayons for me, Brian – give it a really good shake."

As Brian shook the box, Gerald thought he'd play some Bill Haley and the Comets first.

"Do I now take your blindfold off you, Uncle Gerald?" asked Brian, and Gerald nodded, so Brian undid the blindfold.

"So, kids," said Gerald. "I now just need to say the magic word, and then I'll be able to tell you what colour the crayon was."

Gerald moved his arms around in a theatrical way, chanting 'abracadabra'.

"The crayon was…

"GREEN!"

The children gasped – then ran over to Gerald to ask him how he'd done it.

"I couldn't possibly tell you how I did it," teased Gerald, revelling in his glory. "Now, what music do you think we should have on? I'm thinking some rock and roll?"

"I can tell you how you did it."

No-one heard the boy who'd been filming the trick, so the boy raised his voice.

"I CAN TELL YOU HOW YOU DID IT!"

"Sure you can," snapped Gerald, spinning round to face the boy.

"I filmed you in slow motion, and hereby present the following evidence," said the boy, before clearing his throat and continuing. "After Ola placed the crayon in your hand, you turned back round to face us – and, while pointing at the blindfold on the table with your free hand and diverting our attention, you opened your other hand ever so slightly and scratched your thumbnail into the crayon. A few minutes later – after Brian had removed your eye cover and while you were flailing your arms around shouting 'abracadabra' – you sneakily looked at your nail and saw the green wax. Simple."

The children all fell about laughing, but it was Gerald's wife, sister and brother-in-law who laughed the hardest.

"I think young Elliot's got you there, honey," said Gerald's wife.

"I think he might have," agreed Gerald, finally seeing the funny side.

That night, Gerald went to bed with a very sore back.

"Contentment, wealth and fame. Let's draw straws."

"I choose wealth," said the foetus with the longest straw. "With wealth, I can buy whatever I want, do whatever I want and go wherever I want."

The foetus with the second longest straw plumped for fame. "With fame, I will be loved and admired by millions of people."

"Oh," said the foetus with the shortest straw, disappointed. "That means that I'm left with contentment."

* * * * *

"You must be so proud of them, Mary," said Mary's friend. "Little Colby, eh?"

"I am," said Mary. "And, yes, Colby's on this year's rich list, would you believe?" However, she also knew that her son was close to having a nervous breakdown, as he rarely slept, and she couldn't even remember the last time he'd had a holiday – probably sometime before his divorce. She'd suggested that Colby step down as CEO, or take a sabbatical, but he'd refused. Colby was wedded to his company…for better or worse.

"And Tom. I remember Tom when he was knee-high to a grasshopper, and now I watch him on the big screen!"

"Yes, Tom's playing a boxer in his next film so is currently spending six or seven hours a day in the gym." Mary knew that Tom was really enjoying spending so much time in the gym because it was one of the few places he could go and not get mobbed. She knew that Tom resented the constant invasion of his privacy and longed to be free.

"And Christina's doing very well, too," said Mary, who found it annoying that her friends never asked about her third triplet.

Christina was a children's book illustrator who lived with her childhood sweetheart, Digby, and their three dogs – Jim, Pete and Dave.

Christina was by far the happiest of Mary's three children.

71

It took the skilled professional a couple of minutes to find a blood vessel from which to draw the man's blood. To find the vessel, she had to probe around underneath the man's skin, but it didn't seem to bother him – he didn't stir.

When she did, eventually, find a suitable vessel, she bit into it and drank for what must have been a good three or four minutes.

Then she flew away.

72

They were to be on the M1 for a long time – from Luton all the way to Leeds.

The first variable message sign that they saw was in Luton, and, rather bizarrely, it read, 'Luton: the town, where many a hat would take shape'.

"What on earth?" wondered Phil, aloud.

"That is really odd," agreed Phil's partner, Leon. "Luton: the town, where many a hat would take shape. What's *that* got to do with the traffic conditions?"

"Loopy Luton," said Phil.

Half an hour later, as they passed junction 14 near Milton Keynes, there was another variable message sign, and this one read, 'MK: the new town, where you're never far from a lake'.

"Are we on drugs?" asked Phil.

"I'm pretty sure we're not," replied Leon. "And it would be bad if we were, given we're police officers."

Fifteen miles later, they passed a third variable message sign, which read, 'Northampton: not a city, but one of the largest towns in the UK'.

"There's something really odd going on here," said Phil, perplexed. "Can you remember the other messages, Leon? We should jot them all down."

Leon grabbed a pen and some paper, and between them they managed to recall the three messages.

"We have – Luton: the town, where many a hat would take shape," said Leon.

"Then?" prompted Phil.

"Then, MK: the new town, where you're never far from a lake. Followed by – Northampton: not a city, but one of the largest towns in the UK."

"I think it's some sort of treasure hunt," said Phil.

The next odd sign, or clue, came at junction 20 – where, rather than it saying something like 'twenty minute delays expected from junction 22', it said, 'Rugby: the birthplace of the sport Webb Ellis was first to play'.

After coming across the next peculiar sign, which read, 'One of the oldest cities in England, Leicester lies on the River Soar', the off-duty police officers started to speculate how someone might have managed to hack into all of the signs. *Were the control boxes really that insecure? Was it really that easy to change the code?*

As the officers got closer to Loughborough, they guessed that a sign here would probably talk about Loughborough's sporting pedigree, and they weren't disappointed – the sign just before junction 23 read, 'Loughborough boasts a university, where sport is at the fore'.

After passing the sign at Loughborough, Leon rang his boss at Bedfordshire Police and reported the hacking – and, duty done, he and Phil were intrigued to see what any further tampered signs, or clues, might say.

At Birmingham, the variable message sign said, 'Aston Villa or Birmingham City – a key choice each Brummie must make'.

"This is so bizarre," said Phil for the thousandth time that day.

Then, minutes later, they were informed that 'Lady Godiva trotted around Coventry, Leofric's taxes too much to take'.

As they neared junction 25, they came across a sign telling them that 'Nottingham's Robin Hood would rob from the rich and give to the poor'.

"You kind of guessed they'd mention Robin Hood here," said Leon.

"Yes," agreed Phil.

A couple of minutes after the Robin Hood sign, they were informed that 'The Industrial Revolution brought numerous mills, many of which Derby bore'; followed by, 'Situated within the Maun Valley is Mansfield's Market Place'.

"My godparents live in Mansfield," said Leon.

"I didn't know you had godparents," said Phil.

"Yes, I haven't seen them in years."

Next up was: 'Chesterfield lies at the point where the Rother and Hipper come face-to-face', which Leon jotted down – as he had all the messages – then, 'Known for its steel production, Sheffield lies in the valleys of the River Don'.

The variable message between junctions 34 and 35 read, 'One of Yorkshire's largest towns is Rotherham'.

"Not much on Rotherham," commented Phil.

A couple of minutes later, they were informed that 'Scientists first split the atom in Manchester, Eng-land'.

"I didn't know that, did you?" asked Leon.

"No," said Phil.

Then, just before junction 37, a sign said, 'Former mining town, Barnsley, has many a brass band'. And, ahead of junction 39, another sign said, 'Slow – fog. Use lights'.

"Oh," said Leon, disappointed – and not by the fog.

He was soon cheered up, however, by the next clue – 'Wakefield: a city in West Yorkshire, sits by the Calder's flow'. He scribbled it down. Then, minutes later – 'Bradford was the wool capital of the world a hundred years ago'.

Before exiting the M1 at junction 45, Leon and Phil came across two more mysterious messages. The first read, 'The Royal Armouries in Leeds are a real sensation'; the second, 'We hope your journey up the M1 today has been a poetic education'.

"A poetic education," said Leon. "You couldn't pull over at the next services, could you, Phil?"

When Phil was safely parked up at the service station, Leon read out all of the signs' messages in order...

"Luton: the town, where many a hat would take shape,

MK: the new town, where you're never far from a lake,

Northampton: not a city, but one of the largest towns in the UK,

Rugby: the birthplace of the sport Webb Ellis was first to play,

One of the oldest cities in England, Leicester lies on the River Soar,

Loughborough boasts a university, where sport is at the fore,

Aston Villa or Birmingham City – a key choice each Brummie must make,

Lady Godiva trotted around Coventry, Leofric's taxes too much to take,

Nottingham's Robin Hood would rob from the rich and give to the poor,

The Industrial Revolution brought numerous mills, many of which Derby bore,

Situated within the Maun Valley is Mansfield's Market Place,

Chesterfield lies at the point where the Rother and
Hipper come face-to-face,
Known for its steel production, Sheffield lies in the
valleys of the River Don,
One of Yorkshire's largest towns is Rotherham,
Scientists first split the atom in Manchester, Eng-land,
Former mining town, Barnsley, has many a brass band,
Wakefield: a city in West Yorkshire, sits by the Calder's
flow,
Bradford was the wool capital of the world a hundred
years ago,
The Royal Armouries in Leeds are a real sensation,
We hope your journey up the M1 today has been a
poetic education."

"Well, the gaffer *was* saying that cyber-criminals were
becoming more creative!" laughed Phil.

73

They'd never helped out at a race before, but how hard
could it be? All they had to do was hand out water bottles.

They were stationed behind a table of water bottles in
front of a church, about four miles into the race.

It was a really hot day, so they pulled on their caps to
shield their faces from the sun.

As the elite runners ran past, they each took a bottle of
water, which was unexpected because elite athletes didn't
normally stop for water in six-mile races...but it was a
really hot day.

A few minutes later, the fun runners starting jogging by,
and they, too, each took a bottle.

"We're going to run out of water!" screeched Hollie.
"What are we going to do?"

"I don't know," panicked Fiona. "I reckon there's at

least half the field still left to pass, but there're only a few bottles left."

"I'm going to church," said Hollie.

"What?" said Fiona.

"I'm going to church," repeated Hollie.

"Hollie, what are you going on about? I'm glad that you have your faith and everything, but I don't think that *praying* for water is the way to go right now."

But Hollie was off.

"I'm back," shouted Hollie a few minutes later, hugging an extremely large bowl of water and a stack of plastic cups. "The vicar gave them me."

"Cool," said Fiona as they placed the bowl of water on the table and started filling up the cups.

Quarter of an hour later, one of the back-runners hobbled up to them and stopped to take a cup.

"I'm going to need some sort of divine intervention to finish this race," he joked, and Hollie chuckled while watching him drink the holy water.

74

Lillian, Laurence's sister, loved to play hide and seek, and she'd usually hide in the manor but would sometimes venture outside and find a covert spot in Gestingthorpe's gardens.

Having searched the manor from top to bottom, Laurence guessed that Lillian must be hiding outside again.

"I am just going outside and may be some time," he told his father, before leaving the manor and continuing his search in the sun-drenched gardens.

Two hours passed…

…then a further twenty-five years.

"I am just going outside and may be some time," Oates told Scott, before leaving the tent.

As he took his final, painful steps, Captain Laurence Oates thought back to that glorious summer's day in Gestingthorpe's gardens.

75

"Did you hear how the humans have copied us?" said Mrs Cod to Mr Cod.

"No, do tell."

"They realised that we have antifreeze proteins in our blood that stop us from freezing in icy waters, so they've created a new polymer that they use in blood banks, which stops the blood from freezing and killing off cells."

76

"Whose is the new purple car?" boomed Jim as he burst into the office in his usual flamboyant style. "And *what* is it? Even I can't identify it."

They were a relatively small company, so any new cars in the car park didn't go unnoticed; especially by car enthusiast Jim.

"Not mine," said Lizzie.

"Nor mine," said Ben.

"Ditto," said Frankie.

"Must belong to someone from finance, then," said Jim. "I'll go and ask them."

Jim poked his head into the finance department office. "Guys, whose are the new purple wheels?"

All five of the finance workers looked up, confused.

"Purple?" said Keira. "Guys, have any of you got a new purple car?"

On establishing that nobody had, Jim headed back to

his, Lizzie, Ben and Frankie's office.

"The car doesn't belong to any of the number crunchers," he told his colleagues, "so I wonder if a member of the public's parked it here?"

"Probably," said Ben.

The next day, the purple car was still in the company car park, so Jim went and had a closer look. He found it frustrating that he didn't know what the car was, as he liked to think he could identify every make and model of car. He walked around the vehicle and was struck by how unusual-looking it was, then he crouched down and arched his hand above his eyes to get a better look inside and was baffled by the car's toy-like interior. There was something really odd about this vehicle.

Three days later, the car was still in the firm's car park, so Jim asked Lizzie if they could check out the company CCTV to see who had left it there.

"Nice idea," said Lizzie, "but the cameras don't monitor the car park. If it's still here after the weekend, I'll call the police."

The following Saturday evening, Jim was in the pub with his best friend Andy, and Andy was intrigued when Jim told him about the car and asked if they could go and see it.

As Jim pulled up into the company car park, he was pleased to see that the car was still there. He switched off his lights, and he and Andy jumped out of their car.

"Hhmm, it sure is a strange shape," said Andy, examining the purple vehicle with the aid of the torch on his mobile phone. "And I see what you mean about it being like a toy inside."

The car's lights suddenly came on.

"Must be the owner coming back," hissed Jim, but there was no-one to be seen.

"What's going on?" screamed Andy as the car's aberrant lights suddenly started to flash in a very random way.

"This is weird," panicked Jim. "Really weird."

"Can we go?" asked Andy, feeling very spooked out.
"We sure can," said Jim.

* * * * *

Jim took a sharp intake of breath as he drove into the work car park the following Monday morning and scoured the parking bays. However, the purple vehicle was nowhere to be seen.

"Morning," said Jim, quietly, as he walked into the office.

Jim's quietness was more deafening to his colleagues than his loudness, due to its unusualness, so they all looked up at him.

"Are you okay, Jim?" asked Lizzie. "You look a little pale."

"Like you've seen a ghost or something," said Ben, who noticed that Jim was fixating on the new intern. Granted, she was a little strange-looking, but he thought it very rude of Jim to stare at her in such an intent, almost fearful, way.

"The car's gone." said Lizzie. "And we have a new member of the team, Jim. Let me introduce you to *Liane*."

"Anagram," breathed Jim, before fainting.

77

I was tiny and round to start with; as all of us are. Then I broke the mould and started to grow at a phenomenal rate, becoming long, scrawny and thin.

My appearance didn't get much better in later life, which got me into a spin, so I had to have some downtime.

But I ended my life on a high. I finally realised that I was beautiful. Colourful, intricate, wonderful and beautiful.

Such was my journey from egg to caterpillar to chrysalis to butterfly.

78

In the beginning, it wasn't obvious that they had souls, but their souls had always been there. As an example, certain plants could sense which ants would try to steal their nectar, so they'd close their flowers when these particular ants were around.

Fast-forward a billion years, and the plants' and the trees' souls and physical abilities had evolved considerably.

In parallel, human beings had also evolved considerably, and human travel was no longer limited by the fourth-dimension – time. As a result, the Disaster Eradication Programme (DEP) had been set up so that its officers could go back in time and stop the wars and natural disasters of the past from happening. The only restrictions were:

- *While lives could be saved, those lives could not then spawn new life;*

- *All human, animal and plant babies that were spawned in the original iteration of life had to be spawned by the same parents, and at the same time, in any subsequent iterations of life (this required some sophisticated social engineering, which the Ethics Division often had a lot to say about); and*

- *The current physical environment had to remain the same.*

The aim was to take away the hurt and suffering of the past – and the memories of the hurt and suffering of the past – without changing the present. There was one exception, though. In order to learn from the mistakes of the past and try to stop them from happening in the future, the DEP officers would retain their knowledge and memories of the previous iterations of life.

Unsurprisingly, the millions of years of persecution experienced by the plants and the trees had made them very resentful of the humans – although this resentment would disappear once the DEP had completed its mission – so it was perhaps inevitable that there was an outbreak of war.

The humans won the war, as they had technology on their side, but the trees and the plants caused a fair amount of damage at the start of the conflict because of the trees' greater physical size.

DEP Officer Jiolt Hankman and his family were in the wrong place at the wrong time when the conflict began, and the sight of Jiolt's wife and three children being struck down by the Great Oak – and in such a bloody way – really scarred Jiolt, even though he knew that the DEP would bring his family back to life. His children wouldn't now be able to have children of their own, though.

Post the short war, Jiolt resumed his usual duties in the DEP's Twentieth Century Division, and one Tuesday his brief was to remedy the arboreal damage done by a superbolide that had collided with the Earth in 1908. To do this, he needed to give the relevant instruction to the DEP's Asteroid Impact Avoidance Division.

He never gave that instruction.

* * * * *

In June 1908, a burst meteorite caused an explosion in Siberia that resulted in the destruction of 2,000 square kilometres of forest. Termed 'the Tunguska event', it was the trees' darkest hour.

79

"That was incredible. It must be amazing to be able to play like that."

"It's fun to do the concerts, I suppose."

"I'm sensing a 'but'?"

"But it takes real dedication."

"I can imagine."

"And sacrifices – so many sacrifices."

"But to do what you just did – to be able to play Kaikhosru Shapurji Sorabji's Opus Clavicembalisticum, and flawlessly – is really something. I envy you so much."

"What do you do – sorry, what's your name?"

"I'm Jack, and I work for a large accountancy firm."

"And do you have any hobbies, Jack?"

"I used to, before the children were born. These days, my main hobby seems to be taxi driving."

"But what *were* your hobbies?"

"Hockey was a big one. I still train sometimes, but I don't compete anymore. And I love to dance – tap, modern, ballet – you name it! And I have a passion for craft. The kids and I learnt how to do quilling last weekend; découpage the weekend before."

"That all sounds wonderful."

"But it's nothing compared to what you can do," said Jack-of-all-trades. "You're a master of your craft."

80

"When the match is over, we'll award the trophy to the winning team and play their national anthem – all the verses."

"But–"

"But what, Bruce?"

"I don't think that we should play all the verses of the winning team's national anthem, ma'am, as, if Greece were to win, which they're very likely to, their–"

"It's non-negotiable, Bruce. We'll be playing full national anthems. I want the winning team to be able to stand on the podium for a good few minutes."

"But–"

"But nothing."

"But–"

"Bruce! Stop! Dave – I want full national anthems to be played, is that clear?"

"Yes, ma'am," said Dave, shrugging his shoulders at Bruce.

* * * * *

The day of the tournament arrived, and the two teams that progressed to the final were Croatia and Greece.

"I hope that the Greeks don't win," said Bruce to his girlfriend, Ellie.

"Why?" said Ellie. "I thought you said that Greece was the better team?"

"They are," said Bruce, "but we only have an hour to vacate the arena after the match has finished."

"What's that got to do with anything?" said Ellie, and Bruce muttered something about not asking.

* * * * *

It was 75-74 to Croatia, and there were just three minutes remaining.

"Maybe we're going to be alright after all," sighed Bruce in relief.

Then, in the final minute of the game, Greece got the ball and scored two points.

The whistle blew.

The Greeks celebrated.

Bruce groaned.

As the victorious Greek team climbed onto the podium, their flag was raised and their national anthem started to play.

Half an hour later – the Greek national anthem still going strong – Bruce's agitated boss walked up to Bruce and asked what he'd been going to say that day in the office when she'd cut him off.

"I'd been going to say," began Bruce, wincing, "that the national anthem of Greece has 158 verses."

81

For sale: kite, parachute, base jumping suit, crutches.

82

"Happy Birthday, Chai," said Grandpa Roberts. "It's your special day!"

"Mine and twenty million other people's," said Chai.

83

When my nephew was born; when my niece was born; when Russell proposed to Charlotte…it was you who let me know.

When I passed my exams; when I failed my exams; when I was offered the job…it was you who let me know.

When I got engaged to Richard; when Katy was born…it was you who let people know.

When I lost my bearings in Bristol; when I needed a distraction while waiting at the dentists…it was you who helped me out.

You're my cell mate.

84

He thought himself a genius. And he loved Sprocket. But Sprocket wasn't his – Sprocket was Avril and Alan's, and Avril and Alan were not happy that Sprocket had been spending so much time at the arrogant man's house. They suspected the arrogant man had been feeding her.

One day, things came to a head…

After spending the morning competing in the local crown green bowling tournament, Avril and Alan pulled up onto their drive and saw 'Arrogant Man' standing in his front garden holding Sprocket.

"Sprocket is not your cat!" yelled Avril, striding over.

"No, but is she really yours?" opined Arrogant Man. "Researchers recently concluded that cats – unlike dogs – don't need humans to feel protected; they prefer to look after themselves. So, is she really any of ours?"

"Just hand her over," said Alan.

"To whom?" said Arrogant Man. "As I've already said, the *Felis catus* does not require an owner."

"Very good – you know Latin," said Avril, losing her patience. "Now hand Sprocket over."

"Perhaps we should settle this through a game?" said Arrogant Man. "I'll return Sprocket to you if you can correctly predict what I'll do next."

"What the heck?" began Avril. "You're a nutjob!"

"Hang on, Avril," said Alan suddenly. "Let's play."

Avril looked at Alan, aghast.

"I predict that you won't give us Sprocket back," said Alan.

As Arrogant Man's smug expression transmogrified into shock, Sprocket leapt out of his arms and ran over to Alan.

"Hhmm, it seems that the *Felis catus does* require an owner," said Alan as Sprocket jumped up into his arms. "Oh, and please don't assume that you're the only one who knows about the crocodile paradox."

As Alan carried Sprocket underneath his left arm and used his right arm to steer Avril in the direction of their house, Avril asked Alan what he'd meant by the crocodile paradox.

"Well, if I'd have said that Arrogant Man – what *is* his actual name, Av?"

"I've no idea."

"Well, anyway, if I'd have said that Arrogant Man was going to do anything other than not give Sprocket back, he'd have claimed that he wasn't going to do whatever I'd said he was going to do and would have kept Sprocks."

"Okay, yes, I get that," said Avril, carefully processing what Alan had just said.

"But, by saying that he wasn't going to give Sprocket back, I created a dilemma for Arrogant Man – as, if he were to keep Sprocket, he'd be violating his terms because I'd have correctly guessed that he wouldn't give Sprocket back – so he'd have to give Sprocket back – but, by giving Sprocket back, he'd also be violating his terms because my prediction would no longer be correct, so Sprocket shouldn't be given back. But, if he were to keep Sprocket, he'd be violating his terms because I'd have correctly guessed that he wouldn't give Sprocket back…and so it goes on…we're at an impasse and we have a paradox, and that paradox is called the crocodile paradox."

"And it's a paradox that Arrogant Man wouldn't have expected us stupid people to know!" said Avril.

"Precisely," grinned Alan.

85

Lots of people like Christmas, and Millie and Sarah were no exception. However, for them, Christmas seemed to take an age to come around – perhaps because a year still constituted a large portion of their lives to date.

Every year in late November, Millie and Sarah's mum would buy an Advent candle, and the girls loved these candles – and this year's was deep purple with a cinnamon scent.

Every morning at eight o'clock, Millie and Sarah would congregate in the kitchen, and their mother would light the candle and keep it burning until it got to the point where it displayed the new number of days left until Christmas Day.

* * * * *

On the evening of Friday 4th December, Millie and the other Brownies learnt how to strike a match, and Millie was a natural, picking it up in no time.

The next morning at eight o'clock, Millie, Sarah and their mother gathered in the kitchen to burn down the Advent candle, and the candle filled the air with a warm, spicy and vanilla-like scent.

That evening, after Millie and Sarah's mother had gone to bed, Millie sneaked into Sarah's room and tugged at her sleeping sister's hair.

"Sarah," she trilled, excitedly. "Do you want Christmas to come sooner this year?"

"Oh yes," mumbled Sarah, waking up. "But how?"

"I know where mummy keeps the matches – I watched where she got them from this morning – and Brown Owl taught me how to strike a match, so we could burn down the Advent candle to make it Christmas Day tomorrow."

Sarah's eyes lit up, and they both tiptoed down the stairs

to the kitchen – and, once there, Millie grabbed the matches from the cupboard that she'd seen her mother get them from and struck a match and lit the Advent candle.

Four hours later – the candle still burning – Millie and Sarah were getting very sleepy, and Millie looked up at the clock and saw that it was four a.m.

An hour later – the candle having finally burnt down to '0 – Christmas Day' – Millie and Sarah crept back upstairs to their bedrooms, yawning.

The next morning at eight o'clock, Millie and Sarah's mother was expecting to find her daughters waiting excitedly in the kitchen…but they were nowhere to be seen. She looked at the candle and breathed in the warm, spicy and vanilla-like air.

Millie and Sarah eventually woke at five p.m. and trundled downstairs for breakfast, not realising the time.

"It's five p.m.!" scolded Millie and Sarah's mother when the girls sat down at the table.

"We've missed most of Christmas," sobbed Sarah, which set Millie off.

"Now now, girls," said their mum, consoling them and assuring them that they hadn't really missed Christmas. She then went on to berate them for their night-time adventure.

86

Knowing that it was far more edgy to spend university vacations in the Third World, Mugendi and Thani booked their flights and had their jabs.

On disembarking the hypersonic jet, they experienced a mixture of excitement and trepidation before taking their first steps in the former United Kingdom.

87

"I'm just not very lucky," said the man.

"On the contrary, you're incredibly lucky," said the man's best friend, the actuary.

"I'm lying here in hospital, having accidentally ridden my motorbike into the back of a truck that just happened to be crammed full of mackerel. However, none of this mattered because, while being stitched back up, I thought I'd finally met the girl of my dreams – the Goddess-like nurse. So I chat to her and try to impress her, hoping she'll ignore my fishy smell. But do I manage it? No, of course I don't. Because, instead of impressing her, I vomit all over her. A proper chunder blunder. But you tell me I'm lucky?"

"Yes, you were born."

"Big wow. I'm pretty sure lots of people lucked out there."

"Some say that the odds of you being born – as you – are about one in 400 trillion. A trillion's hard to visualise, though – so, to help, a trillion seconds is equivalent to 32,000 years – so, 400 trillion seconds is equivalent to 12,800,000 years. So, the chance of you being born – as you – is equivalent to one second in 12,800,000 years."

"So I'm pretty lucky, then, really?"

"Yes, you're pretty lucky."

"Thanks, mate."

"Pleasure, mate."

The actuary put the peg back on his nose.

88

For sale: road bike, cycling bib, cleats, baby grow.

"To be or not to be: that is the question:
  Whether 'tis nobler in the mind to suffer
  The slings and arrows of outrageous fortune,
  Or to take arms against a sea of troubles
  And by opposing end them. To die – to sleep,
  No more; and by a sleep to say we end
  The heart-ache and the thousand natural shocks"

And then – hundreds of pairs of eyes staring down at him – Dominic couldn't for the life of him remember what came next, despite having delivered the famous soliloquy dozens of times before.

While Hamlet's contemplating suicide, he thought, *I'm actually committing it. Career suicide. This could be game over for my acting career.*

A huge crash.
Dominic jumped.
The audience jumped.
Part of the set at stage left had toppled over.

"The heart-ache and the thousand *and one* natural shocks," resumed Dominic.
The audience tittered.
"That flesh is heir to: 'tis a consummation
Devoutly to be wish'd. To die, to sleep;
To sleep: perchance to dream: ay, there's the rub;
For in that sleep of death what dreams may come."

* * * * *

Dominic James was the consummate professional, read the review in the newspaper the following day. *He calmly dealt with a scenery mishap during the famous Nursery Scene Soliloquy by masterfully knitting in a brief moment of humour before continuing to deliver the hallowed lines with punctuated pauses that conveyed Hamlet's indecision beautifully. While James got through the ordeal with his head held high, the same couldn't be said for Heidi James, the stage and set manager.*

Dominic put down the newspaper and turned to Heidi and kissed her.

90

The British Royal Family had always been hounded, but when it got to the point where all of their lines of communication had either been hacked or compromised in some way, they could stand it no longer.

The meeting took place at Buckingham Palace, and King William explained to the Head of MI5, Jilly Jones, that there was now no way that he or the other members of his family could safely send each other private messages, so he was keen to discuss whether there were any new and impenetrable modes of communication that they could use.

As King William awaited Jilly's response, he prepared to be blinded by science. Perhaps she'd suggest that his family use some sort of long-distance quantum encryption network.

"Pigeons," said Jilly, finally.

"Er…what?" stuttered the King.

"Pigeons," repeated Jilly.

King William didn't know what to say, so he pretended to do up his shoelace, which was a challenge given he was wearing slip-ons.

Sensing the King's discomfort, Jilly elaborated.

"We're living in a world, sir, where all of our

communication channels are penetrable, as the hackers will always overcome whatever encryption challenges we set them. So, rather than looking to the future and trying to outwit the hackers with emerging technologies and what we believe to be unbreakable codes and algorithms, I think we should look to the past."

A look of understanding started to form on William's face, and he stopped trying to tie up his imaginary shoelace.

"In the First World War," continued Jilly, "pigeons proved to be an extremely reliable – and safe – way to send messages, so why don't we eschew technology and go with this tried and tested method instead?"

"I'm game," said William, nodding enthusiastically.

"Pigeons aren't." replied Jilly. "Not if you're to believe the 1831 Game Act."

William looked uncomfortable again, but reasoned that being Head of MI5 must be a very stressful job.

Following King William's meeting with Jilly, the Royal Family became the proud owners of a number of pet racing pigeons, which was easy to explain away because William simply stated that 'pigeons were the new corgis', and no-one blinked an eye.

Over the following three years, the Royal Family used the pigeons to send each other messages, and it was wonderful to have a safe way to communicate again.

However, this bliss came to an end on 6th May, 2039, when King William was brought his morning e-newspaper.

Prince Harry teases King William for wearing odd socks at the State Opening of Parliament, read the headline.

No Harry hadn't, thought William, *and, anyway, I didn't wear odd socks at the State Opening of Parliament.*

He looked at the accompanying photograph.

Oh darn, I did.

William went on to read that his brother had allegedly sent him a message saying, 'Time for an eye test, bro?'

Later that day, Prince Harry arrived at Buckingham Palace to take tea with his brother, and when William shared his concerns that the media were making up stories again, Harry turned the colour of his hair.

"Harry?" said William, quizzically.

"Er, I think we have a problem, Wills – as, well, I *did* actually send you that eye test message. I sent it via Ernie."

"Hhmm, this is really odd," said William, stroking his beard.

"Like your socks," said Harry.

William asked a courtier to bring Jilly Jones to the palace, and, at the subsequent meeting, he, Harry and Jilly discussed what might have happened. They wondered if Harry's message had maybe fallen off Ernie's leg, but Harry was sure that he'd strapped it on very carefully – and he also pointed out that they hadn't seen Ernie since he'd flown him, so they wondered whether Ernie, as an elderly bird, had maybe died en route. Someone could have easily found the note tied to Ernie's corpse and somehow decoded it.

After an hour or two of theorising, they accepted that they would probably never know what had happened to Ernie – but, from now on, only pigeons under the age of seven would carry notes.

Over the following years, there were no more truthful revelations about the Royals – there were plenty of untruthful revelations, but that was just normal – so King William became convinced that whatever had happened with Ernie had been an anomaly.

Then 2063 happened.

In April 2063, the Royal Family had the shock of its life when an e-book was published, and went viral, that featured a large number of the family's private pigeon messages. How this happened, no-one knew...not until the beginning of the twenty-second century when Jack Fringe published his memoirs.

Jack had been an amateur falconry-handler and a hobbyist cryptographer, and he'd also been the butler at a number of British palaces and castles.

91

Grandpa Roberts was reading his grandson's school report.

'It's important that Chai does things in the right order', was one of the comments from Mrs Jamieson, Chai's teacher.

Grandpa Roberts saw that Chai had scribbled something below this comment.

If the frist and lsat lterter of ervey wrod is in the ceorrct pclae, we can raed any stencnee.

92

It only took a couple of minutes to walk through the town of Squidgeley, and then we were out in the countryside.

One Sunday, we enjoyed a fifteen-mile ramble, and towards the end of our ramble darkness started to set in, so we upped our pace. We passed a couple of other walkers and smiled and said hello; then we passed an elderly-looking man who doffed his cap and grinned at us, and we grinned back.

The grass underfoot suddenly turned to tarmac as we arrived back in Squidgeley, and we passed a friendly-looking middle-aged couple with walking poles.

Silence.

93

They were an inseparable trio – Jamal, Heather and Roger. The Three Musketeers. The three friends who'd grown up together.

During the year that they all turned 17, they went on a trip to Paris together, and it was during this trip that Jamal asked Heather if she'd be his girlfriend – an offer she accepted.

To commemorate their new relationship, Jamal bought a combination padlock and scratched his and Heather's initials onto it, before clipping it on a railing near the Eiffel Tower. As Roger watched Jamal doing this, he couldn't breathe, and it took all of his willpower not to howl out in dismay.

With time, Roger found peace and moved on with his life, but he knew that a part of him would always love Heather.

Eight years after the Paris trip, Roger arranged to meet Jamal and Heather during a weekend when they were all back in their hometown, and as Jamal and Heather entered their chosen restaurant, Roger could tell that something was awry.

When Heather was in the restroom, Jamal told Roger that he'd met someone else and was going to end things with Heather. And, when Jamal was in the restroom, Heather told Roger that she'd fallen out of love with Jamal and made a cryptic comment about locking herself to the wrong man many years ago.

The following weekend, Roger landed at Charles de Gaulle airport, and, after finding his hotel and dumping his suitcase in his room, took the Metro to the Eiffel Tower, before heading to where he vaguely remembered the railing to be.

After an hour's search, he found the lock and calculated that there were 1,000 different permutations and started at 000.

After a couple of hours – and wishing he'd started at 999 – he tried 865, and the lock opened.

Three months later, and two months after Jamal and Heather's break-up, Roger invited Heather round to his place, and, when the moment was right, got down on one knee and gave her a small box.

"Roger, you can't be proposing to me – you're not even my boyfriend!" giggled Heather. However, she played along and opened the box, gasping when she saw the opened combination lock from all those years ago. Roger then swiftly presented her with another box, which contained a new lock with the initials H.B. and R.A.L. scratched onto it.

Two months later, Roger clipped this new lock onto the Ponte Milvio in Rome, then removed the key and threw it in the Tiber, giving Heather a cheeky wink.

94

"Why can't I have you?" he begged. "Everyone else has you – everyone but me. If I had you, I'd feel better and wouldn't be in such a state."

He closed his eyes and tried again.

Hopefully, this time, sleep wouldn't evade the insomniac.

95

"Did you hear how the humans have copied us?" said Mr Humpback Whale to Mr Humpback Whale.

"No, do tell."

"They realised that our fins are lined with small bumps that reduce drag when we swim, so they've lined the blades of their wind turbines with small bumps, which reduces drag and improves performance."

96

Jibu and his mates would often put the world to rights.

* * * * *

After completing his universal relations degree, Givono spent twenty-five years working as a universal policy analyst at a large, Earth-based think tank.

* * * * *

Both Jibu and Givono happened to be walking down the street when the VRNews reporter was out canvassing public opinion, and both men were picked to share their thoughts with the viewing public.

The reporter posed the same question to both Jibu and Givono – "Do you think that going to war with Gamiji is the right thing to do?"

"Yes," said Jibu. "The Gamijian scum are polluting our Earth, and the attack in Antarctica last week means we should blow their planet to smithereens."

The reporter turned to Givono.

"It's difficult," said Givono. "So very difficult. I'm a conditional pacifist, which means that I don't believe in war but accept that, sadly, there are times when war can result in a better, less damaging outcome.

"In the thirteenth century, Sir Thomas Aquinas set out three conditions that were necessary to make a war just: (1) it must be ordered by a competent authority; (2) the cause must be just; and (3) the combatants must have 'a right intention, so that they intend the advancement of good, or the avoidance of evil'.

"If we were to go to war with Gamiji, I'd struggle to know whether conditions (2) and (3) would be being breached or not.

"Yes, the recent attack in Antarctica – which came directly from Gamiji – was troubling and resulted in the loss of a number of innocent Earth lives, but was it a rogue or a state-sponsored attack? And, if we were to attack Gamiji, how many innocent Gamijian lives would be lost, and what would happen to the many decent Earth-dwelling Gamijians? However, if we don't retaliate, and if this *was* just the first in a series of planned state-sponsored attacks, imagine a scenario like Antarctica but in a more populous area."

"And how sure are you of your respective views?" asked the reporter.

"Why are we even having this debate?" said Jibu. "Attack Gamiji right away and let me and my mates deal with the Gamijian scum here on Earth."

Givono, wincing at Jibu's comments, said, "Unlike Jibu, who seems to have great confidence in his beliefs, my level of uncertainty is high. Sky high. Do we use great force to mitigate a chance – which might be an incredibly slim chance – that the Gamijians will use great force on us? And does the Antarctic attack provide us with sufficient evidence that our peace accord with Gamiji means nothing to Gamiji's ruling bodies? As it stands, it's an impossible decision to make, and I think that there at least needs to be an attempt to converse with Gamiji's leaders before any action is taken."

Givono felt the laser strike his head.

"Pompous pillock," laughed Jibu, putting his gun back into its holster and kicking Givono's corpse.

The VRNews reporter ran.

Sir Thomas Aquinas turned in his grave, fearing that, once again, his first condition was about to be breached.

97

For sale: umbrella, raincoat, waterproof trousers, wellington boots, the essential guide to emigration.

98

I had half an hour to kill before she was due to arrive, so I sat on one of the station benches and watched the world go by.

I could see a train in the distance, and a couple of minutes later it was right in front of me, spilling out a wave of passengers.

Keiran loped off the locomotive first; his guitar strapped to his back. Kieran had spent the day at Abbey Road Studios, recording his latest album – an eclectic collection of self-penned tunes that was sure to shake up the music industry.

Ten minutes later, another train arrived, and Niall – a tall, toned pro-tennis player who'd spent the day at Wimbledon – got off. Niall swung his racket bag over his shoulder and jogged to the car park, where his Porsche was waiting for him.

The next train to arrive contained a backpacker called Finn. Finn had a couple more days left in the UK, then he'd be embarking on the South-East Asian leg of his adventure. Finn had been travelling for well over a year now and had been to over fifty different countries.

Then the train that I was waiting for arrived, and a couple of passengers disembarked, but she wasn't one of them. Where was she? And then I saw her – how could you miss her, she was so tall, radiant and beautiful. She spotted me, smiled and ran over.

I felt a hard tap on my shoulder.

"How was your day, shorty," squawked Wendy, my overbearing mother. "Did you finish cleaning Mr Leyton's drive?"

"Hello mum," I muttered, watching the beautiful young woman embrace the equally-handsome young man. "Yes, I did."

My mum and I walked over to the railway station car park, and I drove us home in my old banger.

99

As she watched the tank embark on its maiden voyage, she felt a sense of pride and satisfaction. It moved well over rough terrain and kept a decent speed.

"Nicely engineered," said the consultant.

"Thanks, dad," she replied. "And thanks for the cotton reel."

100

Every morning during the summer of 2011, he'd wake to the trill of his alarm clock and groan. Getting ready for this job was a real production.

After having his breakfast, he'd take off his pyjamas and start painting. He'd paint his legs first – followed by his torso, arms and face – and then he'd call for his girlfriend, Harriet, who would fall out of bed, drag herself down the stairs, pick up the brush and paint Eric's back, usually without saying a word. She'd then put the paintbrush down, let out a yawn and head back to bed.

All painted, Eric would wind the blue toga around his body, then spray his hair. His hair was usually still blue from the day before, but he was a perfectionist and didn't want even a strand of his blond locks to show through.

Thoroughly blue, and in his case not just because of the early start, he'd shout goodbye to Harriet, then leave the house for work.

Walking into a city as a blue Roman was an interesting experience, and Eric would usually be the butt of some Smurf-related joke, which had started to wear a bit thin. However, he never forgot certain moments, such as the schoolgirl's conversation with her friend…

"Did you see that man?"

"What man?"

"The man who turned up out of the blue."

The friend then clocked Eric, and the two girls dissolved into fits of giggles.

And there was the time that Eric had had the disagreement with the man who'd thought that Eric shouldn't be skateboarding on the pavement (on the days that Eric was running late, he'd skateboard into the city).

"It's not safe to use that thing on this busy street," said the man, pointing at Eric's skateboard.

"But I'm being very careful."

"Look, you can argue with me until you're blue in the face," fumed the man, "but skateboards shouldn't be used on busy pavements."

To this day, Eric didn't know whether the man had meant to use that particular turn of phrase or not.

There were two spots in the city that Eric would use – one being a fountain – and there was a wall around the fountain that Eric would sit on.

For hours.

Motionless and silent.

Certain tourists would touch, tickle or goad Eric – trying to make him move, laugh or talk – but he never did.

Eric had always loved a challenge, and he liked proving people wrong. Thus, at the end of the summer of 2011, he could finally put the comments that his teachers had once written about him to rest.

Eric needs to calm down. Eric needs to learn the art of sitting still. Eric needs to get some focus.

101

"So, children, 'one' is the first number, and 'a' is the first letter," said Mrs Jamieson to the class.

"Yet 'a' doesn't feature until the thousandth number," whispered Chai to Leo – who, as usual, had absolutely no idea what Chai was going on about.

102

"Try the new keyboard out," he urged. "See if it's comfortable."

The svelte queen amazed her people by jumping out of the white jack-in-a-box, she typed.

"What did the quick brown fox ever do to you?" he asked.

"He jumped over the lazy dog," she replied. "He should have skirted around him."

"But that wouldn't have worked," he reasoned. "Unless the quick brown fox had skirted around the lazy, jaded dog on the pavement."

"It's not just the brown fox that's quick," she said, typing out this new sentence to check that it contained every letter of the alphabet.

103

She'd always been fascinated by clouds.

As a child, she'd spent many an hour lying on her back, finding pictures in the watery vapour. There had been the unicorn's head in the cumulonimbus; the giant fingerprint in the altocumulus; and the bird with the enormous wingspan in the cirrostratus.

In her early teens, she started to systematically record the different shapes that she saw. She bought a series of notebooks, and every day at four p.m. she'd sketch the sky as seen from her bedroom window.

It was in her late teens that she started to notice the pattern. On the afternoons before particularly destructive natural disasters, she'd always see fish-shaped stratocumuli; and, on the eves of major terrorist attacks, she'd see triangles etched into cirrocumuli.

She passed her exams at 18 and worked for the summer before leaving home for university. If truth be told, she didn't really want to leave home, as she felt that it was her duty…almost her calling…to be at her bedroom window at four p.m. each day, observing the sky.

A couple of weeks before she was due to leave for college, she knew that she had to speak out; it was almost as if she didn't have a choice in the matter. So she searched the Web for a contact number and gave the government department a call.

A week later, she arrived in the capital and made her way to the listed building, where she sat in the reception – nerves sloshing around in her stomach like clothes in a washing machine – until a suited man appeared and beckoned her into a meeting room.

As she regaled the man with her cloud-based findings, she could appreciate how absurd her hypothesis must sound, but they were living in a world where humankind still didn't know what 95% of the universe was made up of; they were living in a world in which humans hadn't found any empirical evidence to suggest that other life forms didn't exist; and they were living in a world where consciousness was not yet properly understood. So, amidst all this uncertainty, it was imperative to keep an open mind.

She was, therefore, crushed when the man handed her the psychiatrist's phone number. She was crushed that the human race could be so cocksure despite the vast gaps in its knowledge.

* * * * *

During her final term at university, she returned to her family home, and after a particularly intense day's swotting, glanced at her watch and saw that it was nearly four p.m. She hadn't done it in years, as it had been too painful and had brought back the feelings of humiliation, but she was stronger now.

She saw a cirrocumulus with a triangle etched into it.

Oh no, she thought.

However, there was a circle surrounding the triangle – something she hadn't seen before.

* * * * *

Seventy years earlier, on 5th August, 1945, her grandmother had looked out of that very same window and seen a white, patchy cloud with a triangle etched into it...surrounded by a circle.

On 6th August, 1945, the United States Army Air Force dropped an atomic bomb on Hiroshima.

104

After a frenzied sprint, he grabbed it.

The opposing team started to charge at him, so he threw it to his teammate.

The Boxing Day sales were getting more and more physical each year.

105

It was a quadcopter with a built-in camera. As birthday presents went, it was pretty neat. Neil's girlfriend, Freya, had done well.

In the days and weeks that followed, Neil spent many an hour practising his bank turns and attempting to get his drone to hover. And, during one particular session, he accidentally flew his quadcopter over his neighbours', and their neighbours', back garden, which made him curse because he didn't want to be prosecuted for spying.

That evening, on watching back the day's footage, he got to the point where his drone had strayed, and he saw an aerial view of his neighbours' washing line – not very exciting – and an aerial view of his neighbours' neighbours' garden, which contained a large number of long-leaved plants.

"I know those plants," he whispered, thinking back to his student days when he'd become well-acquainted with the herbs.

Neil didn't know his neighbours' neighbours, as he was relatively new to the area, but he imagined that they must be a group of enterprising young twenty-somethings who were harbouring a thriving cottage industry.

He didn't know what to do. As a responsible member of

society, he knew that he should report his neighbours to the police. However, he also believed in giving people second chances, so he decided to go round to his neighbours' neighbours' house, tell them what he'd seen, and give them a chance to disband their illegal operation.

On walking up to his neighbours' neighbours' door and pressing their doorbell, it suddenly occurred to Neil that this was a monumentally stupid idea, as the neighbours could bludgeon him to death with a chair leg or tie him up in their basement for twenty-five years. However, as he started to walk away, the door opened, and it was too late.

An old lady.

That threw him.

"Hello dear, how can I help you?"

Neil's surprise rendered him ineloquent, so he mumbled something about being new to the area and wanting to say hello to his neighbours.

"Oh, how lovely, dear. Do come in."

Given that Neil had just told the lady that he'd wanted to get to know his new neighbours, he could hardly say no now.

As Neil followed the sweet old lady down the hallway and into the kitchen, he figured it out. This must be the lady's grandchild's house, and she must have been house-sitting for them, not knowing that the plants in their garden were cannabis plants. Yes, that must be it.

Neil walked into the kitchen, where an elderly-looking man was sitting at a table.

"Humphrey, this is…what's your name, lovey?"

"Neil."

"Neil's new to the area, Humph, and is keen to meet his neighbours."

Maybe they *were* Neil's neighbours, then?

"Hello young man," said Humphrey, shaking Neil's hand.

"Can I get you a cup of tea, Neil?" asked the old lady, and Neil nodded.

As the lady made the tea, Humphrey studied Neil carefully, which made Neil feel very self-conscious, so he looked out of the window. "What a nice garden," he said, looking at the plantation. "Although I suspect you haven't lived here very long and aren't aware that some of the plants aren't perhaps what you think they are."

The old lady gave Neil his tea – which had an odd flavour – and Humphrey began talking to Neil in a low and strangely mesmerising tone, and the tension eked out of Neil's face.

"From this point on, every breath takes you deeper; and the deeper you go, the better you feel; and the better you feel, the deeper you go."

The next thing Neil knew, he was back in his house and his phone was ringing. It was his girlfriend, Freya.

"Did you sort out your private issue?" asked Freya.

"What private issue?" said Neil, perplexed.

"The mysterious private issue you said you needed to sort out today."

Neil had absolutely no idea what Freya was going on about.

106

The lexicographer was bemused to see that 'coward' was literally in 'a crowd'.

107

Piper was delighted to become a godparent because it meant that she had a little person to play with, without having to own one. As a 'welcome to the world', she decided to present her newborn godson with a list of top tips that she hoped would help him in later life.

- *Never take yourself too seriously.*
- *Don't set yourself limits – especially limits on your imagination.*
- *Know that sometimes it's more sensible to break the rules than follow them (NB: don't show this list to your future teachers or employers).*
- *Feel your way for a while and try new things so you know what you really love doing. And, when you do discover your passions, follow them.*
- *Remember that people should earn your respect by doing what they say they're going to do. However, this doesn't apply when your mummy says she'll have your guts for garters.*
- *Don't be a slave to social conditioning. Do things your way – even, and especially, if that's a new way. Then write a song about doing things your way. I'm sure that's not been done before.*
- *There are two groups of people in this world – doers and critics. Be in the first group, as the second group's overpopulated.*
- *Only ever accept constructive criticism from people who have constructed something.*
- *If you feel for someone who's suffering, tell them, else they won't know that you care. You never know how big an impact your kind words might have.*
- *Don't judge, as you never know what's really going on with anyone, and accept that everyone does things differently, and that's fine. So, when your school friend decides that dressing up as a banana is cool, just go with that. Some of the most interesting people in this world are bananas.*

- *Respect people's dreams and encourage them to dream more. Strong people lift other people up.*
- *Laugh. A sense of humour gets you through everything, and finding something funny is one of the best feelings in the world. However, when you're worried that you're going to laugh at a highly inappropriate moment, hold your breath, bite your inner cheeks and stare at the ground.*
- *If a relationship isn't two-way, it's no way.*
- *Don't ever be bossy or let others boss you around. Bossiness isn't leadership – it's bossiness.*
- *Try to form your views and opinions from primary sources.*
- *Get an appreciation for credible sample sizes (we'll chat about this when you're older (two, maybe)).*
- *Stay away from sanctimonious people (a trillion miles should do it). They're the worst company and, ironically, often the most flawed.*
- *Don't worry about the past or the future. Focus on the now – the present is a gift.*
- *Don't place too much value on material goods, as they're a misnomer. Goods aren't good, just like peanuts aren't nuts. Godparents are nuts, though.*

108

The tools were laid out in a straight line, and he gently caressed them, appearing to be deep in thought.

I sat on the chair he'd put me in, trying to remember the good times.

He then picked up a particularly pointy-looking tool and

asked me to open wide.

109

Ted was out cycling, and it was while pedalling down a particularly narrow country lane that the van passed him. However, the van left Ted with hardly any room, so Ted ended up wobbling. And Ted's wobbling cost him dear – the approaching car hit him head on.

Ted regained consciousness, but everything was a daze. He was lying on tarmac, and there was a man dressed in green kneeling over him.

Ted turned his head to his right and saw another man dressed in green consoling a distressed young woman.

"I simply couldn't have avoided him," she was sobbing. "He was wobbling so badly."

"Don't despair, miss," said the second man in green. "Patrick's got the man breathing again, so I'm sure he'll pull through with no serious damage."

Ted turned his head back to his left and homed in on the first man's name badge: *Patrick Littleman*. He focused on Patrick's face and realised that he knew that face. It was the face of a homeless man he'd once tried to help – a homeless man who he'd wanted to give a job to, but the homeless man had disappeared.

110

On reversing out of the parking space, Tom clipped the neighbouring car's tail light and cursed.

"How on earth did you pass your driving test, Tom?" marvelled Vicky, Tom's girlfriend. "You must have had a very lenient driving examiner."

* * * * *

Tom lined up with all the other competitors. The prize for winning this particular cross-country race was £200, so Tom's family had deemed it worth putting some effort in.

The starter yelled "Go!", and Tom shot off, leaving the rest of the field behind. They didn't panic, though, as they knew that Tom would never be able to maintain such a fast pace.

Tom reached the edge of the wooded part of the course and bolted into the forest, heaving.

Twenty minutes later, he sprinted out the other side.

During the final mile, Tom ran out of steam. However, he was so far ahead of the other competitors, he still managed to take first place and claim the £200.

* * * * *

"This young man definitely stole the coat from our store," shouted the clothes shop owner while pointing at the boy's photograph. "If our CCTV hadn't've been down, we'd have had irrefutable evidence that it was him. We saw him take it, for God's sake!"

"I hear you," said the police officer sympathetically. "I really do. But we have irrefutable evidence that Tom was at football training when you say he stole the coat. His coach and his teammates have all verified it."

"Look, I don't know how he's done it," fumed the shop owner, "but he was definitely the thief, I tell you!"

* * * * *

Seventeen years earlier, when Maggie had given birth to Tom, she and Desmond had had a surprise. That surprise had been Adam.

111

Ally had always struggled to focus. But when it came to this particular challenge, we knew he needed to succeed. Crucial for learning language. Described as the building blocks of literacy. Early mastery was advised. Frank and I spent hours showing Ally flash cards. Great big flash cards. Helping him form the right sounds. I suggested that we teach him a few at a time. Just so he didn't get overwhelmed. Knowing our son as we did. Luckily, Ally started to get the hang of it. Memorising what sound was associated with what shape. Now we were starting to make some progress. Observing him learn the different sounds was exciting. Pairing the sounds with the shapes that would enable him to write words and then sentences. Quite something. Rites of passage such as these were special. So very special. Time flies by so quickly when you have a child. Use that time to enjoy watching them develop. View each milestone as a wonder. When Ally learnt the last of the twenty-six letters, we were elated. 'X, ex, as used in X-ray,' he told us. 'Yes, Ally, excellent,' we said. 'Z, zed, as used in zenzizenzizenzic,' he then said, 'the term that was once used to represent the eighth power of a number.'

Frank and I gasped – Ally didn't know Y.

112

Izzie didn't just read the novel – she *lived* it.

She was with Kellie every step of the way – from Kellie's childhood in the orphanage, through to her youth battling addiction, and during Kellie's twenties when she worked the streets.

Izzie could feel herself physically willing Kellie to have

some luck and find happiness, and happily the author had clearly wanted this for Kellie, too.

In Kellie's thirties, she discovered a latent talent for cooking, and by her mid-forties she'd been so successful she not only ran, but owned, an exclusive restaurant in a trendy part of London.

As a voracious reader, Izzie consumed this latest novel over the course of a weekend, so by Sunday evening she could feel her limbs starting to seize up, which called for a night-time stroll.

After pulling on her boots, she left her flat, remembering to turn off the landing light on her way out.

Halfway through her walk, she passed a scantily-clad woman who was lingering by the side of the road, smoking. The woman absent-mindedly threw her cigarette on the ground, but instead of landing on the ground, it landed on Izzie's boot and burnt through the tan suede.

"You stupid, careless whore!" fumed Izzie, livid. "You've ruined my new boots!"

113

Tony did own a mobile phone, so he wasn't a complete Luddite. However, he rarely used his phone, and he always forgot to carry it around with him. If people wanted to get in touch with Tony, they knew that their best bet was to ring Tony's landline.

On Tony's 80th birthday, his young granddaughter, Posy, forgot about her grandfather's aversion to technology and sent him a text.

Happy b'day g'dad. WUU2 2day? Wud b gr8 2 meet 2 give u ur present. Hope u like it & it m8ks u :) LOL. Posy

As it was Tony's birthday, it was one of the rare occasions when he was actually carrying around, and monitoring, his mobile phone.

On reading Posy's text, Tony wondered whether he'd accidentally switched his phone's default language setting to something other than English. However, he then started to piece the jigsaw together and realised that Posy wasn't talking about basins in which to wash one's nether regions and conflicts from the late 1930s and early 1940s. Instead, she was asking her grandfather if she could meet up with him and give him his birthday present. He had no idea what the LOL meant, though – but, knowing his Posy, he guessed it must be lots of love.

114

"True thoughts," said the scientist to the registrar. "The dissolvable pills will reveal their true thoughts."

* * * * *

"Welcome, Phoebe and Andrew, and congratulations on deciding to get married! So, today I just need to ask each of you a few basic questions about both yourselves and your spouses-to-be – and it's obviously illegal to give any false information. I'll then check your documents – and, after all of this is done, the notice of your wedding will be displayed in our office for twenty-eight days, and then you'll just need to arrange your ceremony! Now, before we get started, let me get you both a drink."

The registrar returned to the room a few minutes later with two glasses of water.

"So, Phoebe, let's start with you. Andrew, if I could get you to go and sit in the waiting room, please?"

Andrew got up and left.

"Okay, Phoebe. Can you give me your full name, please?"

"Phoebe McCourt," said Phoebe, sipping her drink.

"No middle name?"

"'Fraid not."

Why did people always ask her that? She knew what a full name was.

"And your date of birth?"

"18th September, 1986."

"And what do you do for a living, Phoebe?"

"I'm an accountant."

What a cool job this registrar has. She gets to be nosy for a living.

"And now a few questions about Andrew. Firstly, what's Andrew's full name?"

"Andrew Luke Hans Bates."

I mean, really. What were his parents thinking?

"And Andrew's date of birth?"

"5th January, 1987."

Just call me a cougar, why don't you?

The registrar bit her lip, as if she was trying to suppress a smile, then asked Phoebe what Andrew's occupation was.

Oh my goodness, what did he say he did again? Something to do with recruitment. A recruiter? Headhunter? That'd teach her to glaze over when Andrew talked about his job.

"Andrew's a, er, headhunting-recruiter?" said Phoebe, hedging her bets and feeling embarrassed that she didn't know Andrew's formal job title.

"It's amazing how many people struggle with that one," joked the registrar.

Yeah, yeah – she's just being kind.

"So really don't worry about it," reassured the registrar. "And, finally, if you can give me the full names and occupations of both of your fathers, please?"

I don't have two fathers.

"And I obviously mean your father and Andrew's father when I say 'your two fathers'."

"Er, Philip Andrew McCourt. Farmer. And Jim 'maybe-some-middle-name' Bates – I'm not sure, sorry –

engineer."

My goodness. She must think that this is some sort of sham marriage. I don't know what Andrew does for a living, and I don't know his dad's full name.

"That's great, thanks, Phoebe. If you can now go and take a seat in the waiting room – and can you get Andrew to come in, please?"

* * * * *

"It's a bit like 'Mr and Mrs' this, isn't it?" joked Andrew as he entered the office, sat down and had a big swig of water.

Gosh I'm so funny.

"Yes, I suppose it is," laughed the registrar. "Now, to start with, can you give me your full name, please?"

"Sure. It's Andrew Luke Hans Bates."

Geez, why did my dad have to like sci-fi so much? I bet she's never seen the films, though. She looks old and frumpy, so I'm probably safe.

"Your parents must like sci-fi, then?" said the registrar, almost spitting out the words.

Wrong there, then.

"And your date of birth and occupation?"

"5th January, 1987."

I know. I don't look it.

"And I'm a recruitment consultant."

"Thanks. And can you tell me Phoebe's full name, date of birth and occupation, please?"

"Sure can. She's Phoebe McCourt, born 18th September, 1986, and she's an accountant."

Oh my goodness. Phoebe doesn't have a middle name, does she? No, I'm sure she said she didn't.

"And, just one final question. What are your and Phoebe's fathers' full names and occupations?"

"My dad's Jim Charles Bates."

Don't spell out his initials. Don't spell out his initials.

The registrar suddenly coughed. It was a strange cough

– a little strangulated.

"And dad's an electrical engineer. Phoebe's dad's Phil McCourt, and Phil's a farmer."

"And does Phoebe's dad have a middle name?"

"Er, he might have?"

Does he? Does he? It's probably something really embarrassing.

"And can you confirm that, to the best of your knowledge, all of this information is correct?"

"I can indeed."

Why do I feel guilty when I have absolutely no reason to? It's weird how that happens.

The registrar called Phoebe back into the office, then checked through the couple's documents.

"Right then, Phoebe and Andrew – we're done! I hope you have a wonderful wedding…and I hope that it's out of this world, Andrew!"

* * * * *

"Welcome, Amanda and Jason, and congratulations on deciding to get married! I just need to ask each of you a few basic questions about both yourselves and your spouses-to-be – and it's obviously illegal to give any false information. I'll then check your documents – and, after all of this is done, the notice of your wedding will be displayed in our office for twenty-eight days, and then you'll just need to arrange your ceremony! Now, before we get started, let me get you both a glass of water."

The registrar left the room, then returned a few minutes later with two glasses of water.

"So, Amanda, let's start with you. Jason, if I can get you to go and sit in the waiting room, please?"

Jason got up and left.

"Okay, Amanda. Can you give me your full name, please?"

"Amanda Barbara Smith."

"And your date of birth and occupation?"

"24th December, 1978."

"Ah, a Christmas Eve baby," said the registrar warmly.

"Yes, that's right."

"And your occupation?"

"Customer service representative."

"That's great, thanks, Amanda. And now the same questions again, but this time about Jason. Firstly, his full name, please?"

"Jason Jake Kendricks," said Amanda, taking a sip of water.

"And his date of birth?"

12th March, 1965. 12th March, 1965.

"12th March, 1965."

"And his occupation?"

Plant and systems operator.

"Plant and systems operator."

"And, finally, can you tell me your father's full name and occupation, and also Jason's father's full name and occupation, please?"

"Howard Smith. Hotelier."

"And Jason's dad?"

Bob Wesley Kendricks. Bob Wesley Kendricks.

"Bob Wesley Kendricks. Pharmacologist."

"Thanks, Amanda. Can I now get you to go and sit in the waiting room, and can you tell Jason to come in?"

* * * * *

Jason entered the registrar's office and sipped some water.

Christmas Eve, '78. Christmas Eve, '78.

"Okay, Jason. Can you give me your full name and date of birth, please?"

"Jason Jake Kendricks, 12th March, 1965, and I work as a plant and systems operator."

"Perfect, thanks, and you pre-empted my next question about your occupation! Now for some questions about

Amanda. Can you give me her full name, date of birth and occupation, please?"

"Christmas Eve, 1978. Amanda Barbara Smith. Customer service representative."

"Thank you. So…24th December, 1978…which makes her…?"

Gaah! 2,016 minus 1,978. Was that 40? 39? No…wait…wait…

"Thirty-eight!"

"Good. Good. I now just need some information about your father, and also Amanda's father. Full names and occupations, please."

"Bob Wesley Kendricks, pharmacologist. Howard Smith, hotelier, born 12th June, 1950."

"Great, and some additional information there, too! Can I now ask you to go and get Amanda, and, while you do, will you please excuse me for a minute?"

The registrar walked up the stairs to her second office, punching the Home Office number into her mobile phone. As the phone rang out, she mused that it was sometimes so obvious, the mind reading pills weren't even necessary.

115

"Did you hear how the humans have copied us?" said Mrs Firefly to Mr Firefly.

"No, do tell."

"They realised that the jagged scales on our tummies allow us to emit more light and shine more brightly, so they add microstructures to the surfaces of their LEDs, which lets more light escape from them."

116

Everywhere she went, the sheep went too. If she was working in the study, cooking in the kitchen or reading in the lounge, they would always be with her.

When she replaced her sheep with frogs, the frogs were always with her too.

117

He didn't have much time left. Weeks. Maybe days. The immobility was hard, but the blindness was harder because not being able to read was akin to not being able to breathe. He could learn Braille, but it was unlikely he'd attain any sort of fluency before he met his maker, and audio books weren't an option due to his profound deafness.

He scratched his knee and felt the indent.

It'd been the first ski trip he'd ever been on, and he'd spent the majority of his time on the nursery slopes. However, on the final day, he'd attempted a green run, followed by a blue – and it'd been on a steep part of this blue run that he'd lost control and crashed into the woman…followed by the barrier. The woman was fine, but the barrier and his knee were not. However, it wasn't all bad, as, four years later, he married that woman.

The carer put the spoon in his hand and together they lowered it into the broth, then placed it in his mouth. As the warm liquid flowed over his tongue, he felt the usual twinge of pain.

He shouldn't have climbed so high really, but he'd loved climbing, and this particular tree had been so inviting. When he'd got to the very top, he'd called out to his sister, Jenny, and waved at her…but this waving had been his downfall – literally – and he broke his left leg, and, perhaps more surprisingly, split his tongue open.

That evening, after the carer had helped him into his bed, he rested his head on his right hand and felt his thumb and three fingers. He'd left his other finger at the North Pole during his final expedition.

He'd been on seven polar expeditions in total, and they'd all been wonderful – hard, but wonderful. He thought back to the stunning white vistas and the camaraderie of the teams, and he remembered the sense of excitement and the intoxicating feeling of being alive.

Then he closed his eyes.

118

For sale: hive, bee brush, honey extractor, veil, beekeeper's suit (torn), sting cream.

119

There had only been a couple of times in his life when he'd done something, then looked back and wondered why he'd done what he'd done. The first time had been when he'd left his girlfriend. He'd been besotted with her, but had just upped and left one day. Years later, he was shocked to turn on the news and see that this former girlfriend had murdered her boyfriend...and it later transpired that she'd murdered a string of former boyfriends.

The second time that he'd done something, then looked back and wondered why he'd done what he'd done, was when he'd been in the car accident with his father and his youngest sister. He'd dragged both of them out of the car, but had tended to his sister first, even though his father's need had been greater.

Perhaps Bill's actions had been governed by those strange, unknown forces that are often explained away with terms such as 'instinct', 'intuition' and 'sixth sense'?

* * * * *

She had three players, and one was Bill. Her other players were Bill's two sisters.

Like the vast majority of her competitors, she didn't agree with the compulsory game, so her strategy was to let things take their natural course and only occasionally ever intervene. This low-risk approach meant that she wouldn't win, but she wouldn't lose either. And the consequences of losing were not pleasant.

The big risk-takers in the game were the competitors whose players went on to achieve real infamy down on Earth, or the competitors whose players were quickly killed as a result of their murderous actions or intent. The first type of competitor won and reaped the associated rewards; the second lost and faced the unpleasant consequences.

The rules of the Game of Earth:

- *Each competitor has three players.*

- *One hundred points for each of the competitor's players that are still alive after the age of x (x being the life expectancy in the player's country of birth).*

- *Ten points for every direct kill a competitor's player makes (of both other players and earthlings who are not players).*

120

As she looked at the pitiful remnants of the razed house, she couldn't help but sob.

Building your own home was a big undertaking – you had to lay the foundations, complete the rough framing, sort out the dry-walling and install the flooring.

Penny's parents tried to comfort their daughter.

"You did really well, darling, and you went to an awful lot of effort," said her father.

"And it wasn't wasted," added her mother, licking her gingerbread-flavoured lips. "It tasted delicious."

121

"Where is she?" screamed the woman, hysterically.

"She was here a minute ago. She can't have gone far," reassured the woman's husband. "Let's split up so we can cover more ground."

Quarter of an hour later, they reconvened.

"Success?" asked the husband, knowing full well the answer was no, as their four-year-old wasn't with his wife. He looked to his left – a road; then to his right – a theatre, but their daughter was nowhere to be seen. She was lost in the middle of a city – a big, unfamiliar city.

* * * * *

"Stop the performance!" he shouted, jumping up onto the stage.

The performers looked aghast – some fearful – while the audience looked confused…as if they were trying to work out whether this was part of the play or not.

"Stop the performance!" he yelled again. "You have to help me. You have to help *us*."

"Here, have this," said one of the actors, sensing the man's genuine despair.

The man took the proffered microphone and turned to face the audience.

"Please. I'm sorry to interrupt your play, but you have to help me…us…my wife and me. We've lost our little girl, you see. And she's only four. We were looking at the map. Just for a minute–" he fought back a sob "–and, when we looked up, she was gone."

A woman suddenly jumped up onto the stage and grabbed the microphone. "Okay, everyone, my name's Polly, and this is what we're going to do. Everyone grab your mobile phones and switch them back on if you turned them off for the performance."

There was a rustle of activity as people fished around in their bags and pockets for their phones, and while they were doing this, Polly put the microphone on the floor and spoke to the desperate father.

"Do you have your phone on you?"

"Yes," said the father, confused.

"And does it have a recent photo of your daughter on it?"

"Thousands."

"And do you have any social media accounts?"

"Yes – Networker."

"Great. What's your Networker handle?"

"@heathjones78."

"Okay. I want you to post the most recent photo of your daughter onto your Networker feed."

"Now?"

"Yes – now."

Polly picked up the microphone. "Right – everyone who has a Networker account, I want you to follow @heathjones78."

There was an arrhythmic tapping of keys.

"All done? Great. You should now be able to see a photo of this gentleman's daughter. Can everybody see it?"

There was a ripple of nods.

"Great. I now want you to leave the theatre – quickly, but in an orderly fashion – and go and find this girl! Oh, and if you do find her, bring her here – to the stage. Got it? Now go!"

There was a flurry of activity as everyone left the building.

Five minutes passed, and the distraught mother joined Heath and Polly on the stage, having rung 999.

A further few minutes passed.

An empty auditorium.

Thirty minutes later, people started returning to their seats, and Polly frowned, fearing she'd failed the couple.

Five minutes later, the police turned up, and Polly briefed them on her operation, so they left to join the search.

Ten minutes later, the auditorium was half-full and eerily quiet.

Then – suddenly – two teenagers burst onto the stage, sandwiched around a small child.

"Jessie!" shouted Heath, scooping the child into his arms and twirling her around.

Jessie was then prised away from her father by her mother, so Heath picked Polly up and twirled Polly around.

There was a standing ovation.

122

"What can you see?"

"The hunter. You?"

"The bear."

"It's going to be quite a night," said the astronomer.

123

I'd escaped.

And now I was free.

However, whenever I came across anyone, they cowered in fear. I must have become so disheveled I appeared threatening, as people used to stare at me with intrigue and wonder.

I had very basic requirements – just sleep, shelter and food. But one particular meal led to my death.

I was shot.

Shot for simply finding, and eating, food.

Food that I needed to survive.

124

It was a sensation that was hard to put into words, but for a few moments the world felt different.

* * * * *

Captain Jim Haskill flew his F-35 over Dayton, Ohio, and beneath him stood the grey-bronze statues of Wilber and Orville Wright; their heads slightly raised.

* * * * *

As President Obama passed Martin Luther King's granite face and torso in West Potomac Park, King's eyes gleamed ever so slightly in the sun.

* * * * *

Alan Turing's statue had been sitting on a bench in Sackville Park, Manchester, for over fifteen years.

The excitable young software engineer jumped onto the bench, put his arm around Turing, held out his phone and took a selfie.

Later that afternoon, when the software engineer was looking at the subsequent photograph, he was unaware that Turing's head was turned ever so slightly to the left, in line of sight of the phone.

* * * * *

The bronze sculpture of Helen Keller's face, torso and gesticulating hands resided at the back of the Grand Hall, which was packed when the well-known T11 100-metre runner began her talk.

The 100-metre runner talked about her journey from deaf-blind baby to reigning Paralympic champion, and she also talked about her job as a human rights lawyer.

Amongst all the commotion, no-one noticed the Braille transcript sitting within Helen Keller's animated bronze hands.

* * * * *

For a fleeting moment in time, other statues across the world also stirred.

125

He woke to the dawn chorus – an ambrosial cacophony of tropical sounds. The rising sun enveloped him in its warm, comforting embrace, and he just lay – listening and feeling.

He decided to have an early morning bathe, so he sat up, stretched out his arms and his legs and sauntered over to the lagoon.

After weaving his way through the bounteous reeds, he started swimming, and he was joined by a river turtle, so a merry dance ensued. He then went back to his hammock, where he lay – listening and feeling.

The harsh bleep was relentless.

He smashed the small plastic cube with his fist, but five minutes later the sound tore into his soul again.

He rose and he showered, dowsing himself in chemicals – then he dressed and he ate, filling himself with chemicals.

Squeezed amongst a mass of humanity in a tubular tin, he stared at his feet, which were neatly packaged in shiny brown leather.

He walked down the street, observing the cold, hard lines of the asphalt.

He arrived at his desk for the umpteenth time.

He pressed the button on his computer for the umpteenth time.

He was sweating.

Then he felt the warmth and heard the paradisiacal sounds, and he breathed in the redolence of the flora.

It was all okay.

It was just a nightmare.

He was still on holiday.

126

"Discovering these pictures taught us that portraiture was an established art form long before Rembrandt, Van Dyck and Da Vinci came along," chirruped the curator. "And they give us a fascinating glimpse into the ancient world."

The curator asked the group to form an orderly queue so that everyone could walk past each painting in turn.

"The first portrait you'll see is of a woman. A few years ago, scientists used luminescence digital imaging to analyse the painting, and they discovered the extensive use of a copper-containing synthetic pigment – Egyptian blue – around the woman's eyes, nose and mouth."

As Joni and George walked past the painting, Joni lifted up their young son, Alfie, so that Alfie could see the woman too.

"Was she a mummy?" asked Alfie.

"I'm not sure if she was a mummy like I'm a mummy to you, Alfie," began Joni, "but she ended up a mummy."

"These paintings are known as the Fayum Mummy Paintings, son," said George. "When people died in the first and second centuries, their bodies were preserved and became what are known as mummies, and paintings of the dead people's faces were attached to their mummies."

George looked at Joni and winced. He and Joni liked to answer all of Alfie's questions honestly, but maybe this was too much for a five-year-old?

"Oh, right," said Alfie, before asking if he could play on his scooter that afternoon.

* * * * *

Alfie and Jenny had been the best of friends, so when the teacher came into the classroom and told the class that Jenny wouldn't be coming to school anymore, as she'd been very poorly and had gone to a heavenly place far, far away, Alfie hadn't known whether to be happy or sad.

"I'm happy that Jenny's in a heavenly place," he told his parents that evening, "but, even though she's now far, far away, will I still be able to visit her?"

"Jenny's no longer *physically* here, Alfie," said George, gently. "So you won't be able to *physically* visit her again, but you'll always be able to revisit the memories of the happy times that you shared."

"Oh," said Alfie, before asking if he could play on his scooter.

A week later, Alfie's funeral-clad parents told Alfie to

have fun with grandma and grandad, and they promised to be back by the afternoon. As they opened the front door, Alfie shot upstairs to his bedroom, which made them look at each other with concern. However, a few seconds later, Alfie came bounding back down the stairs, and he pressed a folded-up piece of paper against his dad's chest.

"What's this, son?" said George, unfolding the paper.

He then saw the crayoned drawing of Jenny's face.

127

"Emperors are better than kings because we hold sway over larger areas."

"No, kings are better than emperors because we're more colourful."

"But emperors are bigger."

"But kings are nimbler."

"What are they like," said the sea lion.

"I know," said the orca. "Penguins are so competitive."

128

He burst into the bank and opened fire. After an initial few seconds of undirected, panicked shooting, his situational awareness improved and he started locking on to the armed security guards.

He then switched his games console off and took the Tube to his job at the disarmament charity.

129

The Marlborough Sounds reside at the top of New Zealand's South Island and are a stunningly beautiful collection of sea-drowned valleys; their arborous hills rising steeply from the sea around a sinuous coastline of sheltered inlets and secluded sandy bays. These sandy bays are home to a small number of people who live in isolated homesteads and have next to no connection with the outside world...apart from on a Tuesday afternoon, when they're visited by the weekly mail boat.

One Tuesday, Peter, a backpacker who was in the process of circumnavigating the globe, took a ride on the mail boat and met a number of the Sounds' inhabitants – and there were four who he would never forget.

Peter and Tim – the mail boat's captain-cum-postman – moored at the first of the locals' jetties, and they were greeted by an elderly-looking woman with a kind and intelligent face.

"Good morning to you, Hannah, and also to you, Bones," sang Tim, jumping out of the boat and patting a tiny brown dachshund on the head.

When Tim said good morning to Hannah, he also waved, which Peter found a bit odd given that Hannah was only a few metres away.

Hannah beamed at Tim and waved back, then pointed to the sun and grinned.

"It sure is a glorious day," said Tim, smiling and making shapes with his hands. "Let me introduce you to Peter, Hannah. Peter's joining me for the day to see some more of the Sounds, and he's very pleased to meet you and is excited to see your beautiful home."

Hannah turned to Peter and shook his hand.

"Hannah's an artist," said Tim. "She paints the most incredible pictures of the Sounds – they're absolutely stunning."

Tim made some more shapes with his hands, and Hannah signed back, grinning.

"Hannah would be very happy to show you her paintings, Peter, if you'd like to see them?"

Peter responded enthusiastically, so Hannah led the two men – who were laden with parcels – into her house, guiding them to her kitchen, where they placed the parcels on a table. Hannah's eyes lit up when she saw one of the parcels, and she tore it open, beaming when she saw the shiny new paint brushes. Bones also seemed to be very excited by one of the parcels, and – given its smell – Peter could imagine why.

Hannah beckoned Peter to follow her, and she led him into a large studio full of paintings – the most wonderful paintings you'd ever seen. Peter wasn't often moved by art, but these pictures were breathtaking; Hannah had captured the spirit of the Sounds perfectly. When Peter finally finished looking at the paintings, he pointed to himself, followed by his heart, followed by the paintings – and Hannah beamed.

When Tim and Peter cast off from Hannah's jetty, and Hannah's small slice of the Marlborough Sounds, Tim threw a bone onto the beach, and Bones yelped appreciatively.

When Hannah and Bones had disappeared from view, Peter climbed down into the bottom of the boat and saw the three packages that Hannah had given Tim to post. The packages were clearly paintings, and the top one was addressed to the Prince and Princess of Monaco.

The second inhabitant who Peter would never forget was Ataahua.

Peter first caught sight of Ataahua as she rowed her dinghy towards the mail boat; her long black hair dancing in the breeze.

"Hello Ata," said Tim, gently, as he grabbed Ataahua's dinghy and tied it to the side of his boat. "Peter – can you go and find the parcel addressed to Ataahua Ngata, please?"

"Just one parcel today, Ata," said Tim, passing the parcel that Peter had fetched down to the dark-haired girl.

As Ataahua secured the parcel in her dinghy, Tim grabbed a book from out of a cabinet at the front of his boat and passed it down to Ataahua, who took it and gave Tim a nod and the hint of a smile. Peter saw the book's title – 'How to let the world back in'.

That evening, when Peter was back at his motel, he opened up his laptop and googled 'Ataahua Ngata', and up popped a mass of photos of the Maori beauty. He clicked on Ataahua's Wikipedia entry and learnt that she was a famous Kiwi singer who'd had a nervous breakdown and become a recluse.

The third inhabitant who Peter would never forget was Bob.

Tim tied the mail boat to Bob's jetty, then led Peter to Bob's private Pacific paradise – Bob's small slice of the Marlborough Sounds.

Tim knocked on Bob's door, and it was opened by a large man with a ruddy complexion, who invited Tim and Peter in and offered them a drink.

As the three men sat sipping their drinks in the glass-panelled lounge at the front of Bob's house, they were gifted to a magnificent vista of vast green hills protruding from cerulean waters. Peter asked Bob if he ever felt lonely living in the Sounds, and Bob said that he didn't because his children would often visit – and he also told Peter that Tim would always deliver his mail last so they could enjoy a game of cards and indulge in a glass or two of something strong.

The fourth and final inhabitant who Peter would never forget was Tim. Tim wasn't just a postman – he was a counsellor; a lifeline; a pet lover; a friend; a man who'd learnt Makaton so he could converse with Hannah; a man who was trying to help a beautiful, yet lost, young woman find her way back into society.

Tim was family.

130

He was paralysed.

His eyes were rolling, and his throat had narrowed.

But he came through it.

Just as he always did.

Just as he and eight billion other people always did every time they woke up.

131

"Six whole weeks off school, eh, Chai?" smiled Grandpa Roberts, remembering how much he'd enjoyed the summer holidays when he was a boy.

"It's 10 x 9 x 8 x 7 x 6 x 5 x 4 x 3 x 2 x 1 seconds," replied Chai.

"Yes, lad, I dare say it is."

132

He'd spent weeks planning it, and the key was to get the logistics right. He needed to make sure that Jack didn't turn up until three p.m., by which time everybody would be there.

At two fifty-five p.m., most of the guests were carefully tucked away behind Kit's sofas, although Mike, who was never one to follow the crowd, had crawled into Kit's loft.

The doorbell rang, and Kit opened the door and invited Jack, his best mate, in.

As Jack walked into Kit's lounge, everyone jumped out

from behind the sofas, detonating their party poppers and blowing their horns. Kit then released the loft hatch and Mike fell out, screaming 'Happy Birthday, Jack!'

Jack was made up. He'd thought that it was just going to be him, Kit and Mike playing cards and having a takeaway, but here were all his friends, and there was food, drink, a big pile of presents and a huge cake. Party on! This was a great thirtieth birthday!

Eight months later, it was Kit's big day, and he'd been told to arrive at the Cat and Carriage at one p.m., and he strongly suspected that Jack was about to get his own back.

As he walked into the pub, he scanned the horizon for evidence, but could only see Jack.

"Happy Birthday, mate," said Jack, handing Kit a battered card. "Oh, and I'm afraid Mike's sick so can't make it."

Yeah yeah, 'Mike's sick', thought Kit, wondering where Mike was going to spring from this time.

Half an hour later, Kit and Jack finished their meals, and then Jack had to shoot off to see Tasha, so Kit spent the evening alone.

133

He'd always been a spoilt cat.

When Leila and Rich had bought him as a kitten, it had felt like all of their Christmases had come at once, they'd wanted a pet for so long.

Deciding upon a name for their pride and joy had been a real challenge, but they eventually settled on Hotdog. Why on earth you'd call a cat 'dog', Hotdog would never know, but he could totally understand the 'hot' part, as he'd seen the way that the girl cats in the neighbourhood looked at him.

Every week, Leila and Rich would buy Hotdog a new

toy, and if they wanted to make him really happy, they'd buy him a toy laced with catnip. My, how Hotdog loved catnip.

So, in summary, life was pretty wonderful for Hotdog.

Until the arrival.

Sally-Louise was her name, and she was a lot like Leila and Rich – just smaller and podgier, and she cried a lot. She wasn't furry and nice to stroke, like Hotdog was, and she didn't nuzzle up into Leila and Rich's arms, like Hotdog did. So Hotdog couldn't see what all the fuss was about. But fuss Sally-Louise Leila and Rich did.

And all the time.

Gone were Hotdog's weekly toys. Gone was his freedom to roam around the whole of the house. And gone was his endless supply of cuddles. So he started to spend more time outside, as he still – obviously – got a lot of attention from the girl cats.

* * * * *

Mary lived in a tiny cottage at the edge of the village. It had been three months since Wilf, her husband of forty years, had passed away, so she knew she needed to get back out into society, but she just couldn't bring herself to leave her house.

* * * * *

One particular Tuesday, Hotdog decided to roam further than he'd ever roamed before, and he found himself at the edge of the village.

"Oh, what a beautiful cat," gushed Mary, spotting Hotdog.

Hotdog couldn't disagree with her there.

"Come here and let me stroke you, handsome feline," said Mary, putting down her garden shears.

Hotdog obliged, and spent the next half hour being

patted, petted and thoroughly appreciated. He purred so loudly, he sounded like a car engine.

The next day, Hotdog returned to Mary's house.

And the next.

And the next.

And the next.

One time, Hotdog turned up at Mary's cottage after fighting with another cat who should have known better, and Hotdog's scruffy appearance made Mary wonder whether Hotdog was a stray. "Do you have a home, beautiful boy?" she cooed while tickling Hotdog's nose.

Now, as well as being God's gift to female cats, Hotdog had a decent head on his furry young shoulders, so the germ of an idea started to form...

* * * * *

Leila and Rich were concerned that Hotdog wasn't eating much, but they didn't dwell on it, as they were too busy changing nappies, blending food and giving Sally-Louise baths.

* * * * *

As the days passed, Hotdog became leaner, and Mary became more and more convinced that Hotdog was, in fact, a stray. So, one particular Wednesday, Mary walked to the village shop with more heart and purpose than she'd had in months and bought a few tins of cat food.

* * * * *

When Hotdog hadn't been home for a couple of days, Leila and Rich were concerned...and, when a couple of weeks then passed, they both accepted that, sadly, Hotdog must have been hit by a car.

* * * * *

The following year, Leila, Rich and Sally-Louise were in the village store when Mary walked in. They didn't really know Mary, but they knew that Mary's husband had died a while back, and they knew that Mary had kept a very low profile ever since.

"What an adorable child," enthused Mary, looking at Sally-Louise. "How old is she?"

"She's just turned one," grinned Leila.

"And a proper little monkey she is, too," gushed Rich.

"How are you doing, Mary?" asked Leila, gently, knowing what she did about Mary's past.

"I'm well, thank you," said Mary. "I'm looking for a new scented toy for my cat, Adonis." Her eyes sparkled. "Adonis was a stray, and he absolutely loves catnip!"

As Leila and Rich walked back down the lane towards their house, Leila turned to Rich with a quizzical look in her eye and whispered, "I wonder? I just wonder?"

"I thought exactly the same thing," said Rich, grinning from ear to ear.

134

My family and I were sitting around the dinner table, eating, when I was grabbed and dropped in the study.

Why did the ginormous human hands always have to enter the house and break us up?

135

Anyone who was anyone had a pair of Conduit headphones. Some teenagers took up Saturday jobs just to be able to buy a pair; others had to wait impatiently until birthdays or Christmas.

Fifteen-year-old Billy's campaign to own some Conduits started in the summer, but it wasn't until Christmas that he finally became the proud owner of a bright blue set.

Kate and Phil, Billy's parents, had been worried about Billy for a couple of years now. A once polite and charming young boy, Billy had turned 13…and turned violent. His unprovoked attack on his teacher had led to him being 'tagged like a racing pigeon', as Kate had described it while sobbing to Phil. Never in her wildest dreams had she imagined that her son would end up with a bad behaviour tag clamped around his ankle.

Kate and Phil didn't know where they'd gone wrong with Billy. When Billy was born, they'd bought books on how to be good parents, and they'd always tried to support both Billy and his sister – they'd cultivated a happy family environment with an endless supply of love.

What they didn't know, however, was that Billy hated himself. And Billy didn't know that the reason he hated himself wasn't his fault.

Post-Christmas Day, Billy became permanently attached to his Conduits, and people walking past Kate and Phil's house would often hear Phil shouting, "Billy, take off your headphones and come and eat your tea," or Kate yelling, "Billy, take off your headphones and come and say goodbye to grandma."

That summer, Kate and Phil wondered whether they should be worried about the amount of time Billy was spending listening to his music. However, they hadn't failed to notice that, since having his Conduits, Billy had become far less aggressive.

It was during a community get-together that Kate learnt that Billy wasn't the only teenager who lived in his Conduits. Moira, another parent, shared a concern that her son, Oliver, must be surgically attached to his. She went on to say that Oliver had had serious anxiety issues and had struggled to leave the house, but, since getting his green headphones, he'd started to hang out with his friends a lot more. Moira said that she didn't suppose there was a causal link, but it was funny that things had started to get better for Oliver right after getting his Conduits.

Kate couldn't help but chime in to say how Billy, too, had changed since getting his headphones, but she didn't elaborate, as she wasn't keen to dwell on some of Billy's past behaviours.

Paul, another local parent, said that his daughter, Amy, had broken her first pair of Conduits, so he'd had to get her a new pair. Amy had custom-designed this second pair – they were covered in angels – and Paul joked that Amy might come to regret that decision one day. He said that he'd been loath to pay out for another set, but it was the first time in Amy's life that she'd managed to stay focused on something – although he had no idea what she spent her time listening to.

Later that morning, when Kate arrived back home, Billy sat down with her and Phil and told them why he'd hit his teacher.

They went straight to the police.

That evening, exhausted from the harrowing revelations and subsequent events of the day, Kate told Phil about the conversation she'd had with the other parents. Then, while falling into a broken-hearted slumber, she murmured, "It's almost as if the Conduits are linking the kids to…"

136

"Did you hear how the humans have copied us?" said Mr Horntail Wasp to Mrs Horntail Wasp.

"No, do tell."

"They realised that the two whip-like needles at the ends

of our bodies work like a zip and enable us to drill into trees, so they've designed a saw with extra blades at the end that they think could work well in limited-gravity environments."

137

He grabbed a cup from the bottom of the stack with about ten times more force than was necessary, so all the other paper cups came crashing down to the ground.

He turned to see his co-worker standing behind him.

She snorted.

He snorted.

They then both howled with laughter.

It's in moments like this, thought Jeb, *that I really love life.*

138

It attacked me.

I tried to put my fear and the intense pain from its cuffing aside for a second, to think.

Play dead, I decided.

I was sure I'd read that this was the best course of action.

So I fell down and lay on my stomach, clasping my hands behind my neck – but it didn't work, as the black bear swiped me again.

Then I woke.

Two years later, I spotted the same dark eyes staring at me…and then the bear charged.

The bear bit into my thigh, so I screamed and I shouted and I stretched out my arms in an effort to look as large and as menacing as I could. The bear hesitated, so I took the opportunity to punch it in the face, then I ran – faster than I'd ever run before – not daring to look behind.

When I neared my car, I fumbled around for my keys, opened the car door and jumped inside. I then looked around, panting, but there was no bear to be seen.

The thigh wound was so deep, I had to stay in hospital for almost a week. So, to pass the time, I asked for a laptop and started researching dreams.

I learnt that certain researchers postulate that the biological function of dreams is to simulate life-threatening events in order to allow the dreamer to rehearse how – or how not – to deal with similar real-life events.

That certainly seemed to fit.

139

Yolanda knew that being green was never a particularly good look, but especially on the day of an interview. And she really wanted this job

The day before, she'd taken part in the Colour Race – a 10km run in which the competitors are sprayed with powdered paint at the start of every kilometre. It had been great fun, but, try as she might, she hadn't been able to scrub the green hue off her skin and out of her hair.

She looked at her watch and saw that it was eight a.m. Her interview was at eleven a.m. "Control the controllables," she said to herself, bolting out of the house.

She made a beeline for the supermarket's toiletries section and grabbed a hair dye that featured a model with similar-coloured hair to her pre-green hair. She paid for the dye at the checkout and tried to ignore the cashier's impudent stare. However, his rudeness eventually got the better of her, and she launched into a frenzied diatribe about the injustice of it being okay to have little green men but not little green women.

Back home, she massaged the dye into her scalp and was mortified to look in the mirror twenty minutes later and see that her hair was now blue. Temporarily ignoring the blue hair issue, she put on her suit and pulled on some thick, dark tights, which she knew were going to be uncomfortable given it was summer – but better to have sweaty legs than green legs.

The last thing left to do was to cover up her hair, so she pulled on the only hat that she owned and headed outside.

She got into her car, wondering if she should call the company and pretend to be sick – in truth, she was looking very green – but what if they said that they couldn't re-arrange?

The three interviewers were still scribbling down notes from the previous interview when Yolanda walked into the meeting room, but they stopped and looked up when they heard her scrape back her chair.

"Yolanda," said the Chair, holding out his hand and trying to remedy his open-mouthed, shocked stare. "Yolanda…" he looked down at his notes, "Green."

As Yolanda shook the Chair's hand, she wished with all her heart that her mother had married Mr White.

"I'm Humphry Jones, and these are my colleagues, Gail Hope and John Dean."

"Hello Gail…John," said Yolanda, shaking each of the interviewers' hands in turn. "It's very nice to meet you."

Forty-five minutes later, Humphry posed the final question. "So, Yolanda, what if you've already peaked and have already done your best work?"

"I'm incredibly proud of my professional achievements to date," began Yolanda. "In particular, the way that I handled the aforementioned Hudson Case. However, I'm hungry to learn, and I believe that this appetite for learning, coupled with my burgeoning experience, means that there are great things left for me."

The interviewers all looked very impressed, and

Humphry began wrapping up the interview, thinking it was a great shame that Yolanda had turned up painted green and wearing a ski hat, else she'd have been a shoo-in for the role.

140

It was an artistic masterpiece.

Intricate and beautiful.

The artist deemed it her best piece yet.

And then the human destroyed it with his feather duster.

141

They pulled their masks over their faces and slid their snorkels into their mouths. Then, while treading water, they surveyed the scene. And what a scene it was – sparkling, cyan-blue waters and rolling white beaches.

The garden beneath the sea beckoned, so they flipped up their bodies and faced down. To their left was the edge of the reef – a steep, craggy, white wall teeming with an explosion of multi-coloured, kaleidoscopic activity; to their right, an abyss – a chilling, deep, dark unknown.

They torpedoed down and floated amongst a swarm of brilliant blue and Mikado yellow triangles; such vivacious colours that made them think of the well-known Swedish flat-pack furniture store. It's odd how the mind associates sights; this wasn't the romantic parallel they were hoping for. The delightful three-sided polygons danced around them, bobbing and playing.

They swam back to the water's surface, keeping their heads facing down while gulping in air, as they were loath to break their connection with the Elysian oceanic universe.

Oxygen replenished, they dove into another shoal; each shoal member sporting deep orange stripes accentuated by neighbouring brilliant white stripes.

The shoal suddenly parted when a much larger organism appeared.

Oval and swimming quickly with teeth bared, the organism torpedoed beneath the snorkelers, who hurried back to the water's surface.

Heads bobbing above the water, the snorkelers surveyed the scene. And what a scene it was – sparkling, cyan-blue waters and rolling white beaches.

Down the snorkelers went again, and they were passed by a flash of luminous pink, followed by a group of oversized floating humbugs. A glance to their right revealed a shadow – a shadow impressed upon the cold, dark nothingness – and, fearful of this unknown within the great unknown, they bolted back to the surface. And what a scene it was – sparkling, cyan-blue waters and rolling white beaches.

142

"I've got to go," said Michael, putting down his phone.

"Again?" said Catherine, disappointed. This was Mike's second emergency call of the day, and on a Sunday as well.

"Sorry, Cath, but it's a doctor's vehicle. You carry on playing Ludo with Simon. You're both thrashing me, so it won't change the outcome."

* * * * *

Having picked up the relevant materials from the warehouse, Michael pulled up onto the doctor's drive and could see the issue straight away – the doctor's car windscreen was sporting a sizeable crack.

The doctor appeared at his front door and walked over to Michael.

"Thanks for this. As I said to your guy on the phone, I can't wait until tomorrow, as I'm on call. I could borrow a neighbour's car, but it's much easier to use my own because I've got all of my medical equipment in it."

"I totally understand," said Michael. "Looks like it was one heck of a stone chip."

"No stone chip," said the doctor, pulling his phone from out of his trouser pocket. "It happened here on the drive last night; someone threw this." He showed Michael a photo of a rock.

"Hooligans," said Michael. "Have they nothing better to do? I assume you called the police?"

"Yes. They came round earlier and took the rock away for fingerprint analysis. Apparently, there's been a spate of incidents like this in the neighbourhood over the past few weeks."

"Yes, we can certainly vouch for that, as we've never been so busy. Are they any closer to finding the scumbag?"

"Apparently not."

"Well, let's hope that they catch him – or her – soon, and, in the meantime, I'm afraid this is going to have to be a full replacement job."

"Yes, the guy on the phone said as much."

"It shouldn't take too long, though – maybe an hour – and then I'd advise that you don't use your car for at least an hour afterwards."

"Right you are. Thanks for this."

"No problem," said Michael, wondering how Catherine and Simon were getting on with the game of Ludo.

Three days later, Michael was out repairing a chip on an old lady's car window when his phone rang.

"It's Catherine."

"Oh, hi Catherine. Look, I can't really talk right now; I'm on a job."

"You need to come down to the police station, Mike."

"What? Why? What's happened? Are you okay? Is Simon okay?"

"Yes, we're both fine, but you need to come NOW."

"Okay, I'm on my way."

Michael parked his van in the car park, then rushed into the police station, wondering what was going on. *Had Cath been mugged? Was Simon alright? Was the house okay?*

Catherine was sitting in the waiting room, so Michael rushed over to her.

"What's going on, honey? You look dreadful."

"I feel it," said Catherine. "Simon's currently in the holding room, and we've been waiting for you to arrive before he gets questioned."

"Gets questioned? Why in Heaven's name is our son getting questioned?"

"Because they think it was him, Mike."

"They think *what* was him?"

"They think Simon's the one who's been throwing rocks at people's car windscreens."

"Simon?" gasped Michael, horrified. "*Our* Simon?"

"Yes, Mike, *our* Simon."

"But that's ridiculous. They must have got their wires crossed. Simon wouldn't do anything like that; he's a good lad."

"That's what I thought, but apparently they have irrefutable evidence."

"But I thought that we'd brought him up properly, Cath? I thought we'd taught him to respect other people's property?"

"I know," said Catherine, forlornly.

* * * * *

Three months earlier:

"I think I'm going to lose my job, Cath."

"Are they laying people off?"

"Yes. They said in a meeting today that half the workforce would be gone by the end of the year. They didn't put it like that – they put it more corporately – but that was the upshot. The demand for car windscreen repairs just isn't there anymore; not since people have been working from home."

"Look, don't worry, Mike. Whatever happens, we'll get through it. We always do."

Simon was sitting at the top of the staircase, eavesdropping his parents' conversation.

143

"I'm just a small cog in a big wheel; no-one would notice if I wasn't here," lamented Sam, the filing clerk.

"In an internal combustion engine, gaskets are very small parts, yet they're essential to the smooth running of the car," said Sam's boss, Ellen. "As well as keeping the car's engine in optimal condition, they help to prevent leaks from joined objects."

Sam spent the rest of the day filing with gusto.

144

"It's broken!" sobbed Christophe, staring at the dropped toy.

Stephan – Christophe's dad – looked exhausted, so Lucas – Stephan's best friend – stepped in.

"Surely it can be fixed, Christophe? It's amazing how things can heal – it's like magic!"

Christophe looked intrigued and stopped crying.

"Maybe it's like my finger, Chris. Look at it." Lucas held out his left index finger. "Looks good, doesn't it? Nice and straight and fully functioning." He bent his finger to demonstrate that functionality. "But, if I were to tell you that, this time last year, this finger was completely broken – broken in two – I bet you wouldn't believe me, would you?"

"No," marvelled Christophe.

"Well, it was. It was completely broken. But, after a few weeks of it being splinted to my middle finger, it was as good as new again. So, maybe we can take the broken pieces of your toy and piece *them* back together, Chris?"

"Can we?" said Christophe, hopefully.

"Maybe. However, if we can't, then that's not a bad thing either. Do you like eggs?"

"I do," said Christophe. "With soldiers!"

"And how do you eat those eggs?"

"I tap them with my spoon."

"Aha – so it's only after breaking them that you get to the delicious flavour?"

"Yes."

"So maybe broken things aren't such a bad thing after all, huh?"

"No."

"And surely nothing's ever completely broken, anyway? Even a broken clock works at two points in the day. So, let's take your toy and see if we can fix it. And, if we can't, we'll enjoy it just as much in its separate parts."

"Okay," enthused Christophe.

As Lucas and Christophe squatted down to pick up the remnants of the toy, Lucas felt Stephan's hand patting him, appreciatively, on the back.

145

It was a rough neighbourhood, so it was unwise to stray away from your patch. Those who did, encountered sabre-rattling, at best, and full-on brawls, at worst.

After Zigzag lost an ear in such a brawl, he never strayed into Fluffball's territory again.

146

"You're in A&E, sir. We have our best doctors working on you."

"Thank goodness," said Humpty Dumpty, "as I don't want the king's horses and king's men working on me."

147

I saw a lot throughout the course of my life.

I lived in the middle of a shopping mall, but don't feel sorry for me. It was a good life, and other members of my family were in far worse positions than me.

One incident that I never forgot involved a young girl. The girl and her mum had been mooching around the clothes store opposite me, but the girl had become restless so had left the shop and sat on the bench in front of the store's window.

I watched the girl for a while. The bench was too big for her, so she was able to swing her legs up and down. I looked to the girl's left – not much going on there – so I returned to the girl, and what a good job I did because she was no longer alone. It's funny, but I often knew exactly where to look; it was a sort of sixth sense I had, and I sometimes wondered whether there was a God watching over me, always pointing me in the right direction.

The girl was with a man who was proffering his hand to her. It looked as though she was going to take it, so I shook my head from left to right and saw the girl briefly look up at me, but she didn't heed my warning, as she took the man's hand and walked off with him.

I wanted to follow them.

But I couldn't.

I couldn't move.

I was paralysed.

A security guard suddenly turned up and rugby-tackled the man to the ground, which made the girl cry.

The girl's mother heard her daughter's sobs and raced out of the clothes shop to comfort her.

I saw all this from the corner of my metal-cased, digital eye.

148

I met her in Heaven. I told her I felt short-changed because I'd died thirty years short of my country's average life expectancy, and she told me she felt blessed because she'd lived ten years longer than her country's average life expectancy. We got on well, no doubt because we arrived in Heaven at the same time and at the same age.

149

For sale: quarter-sized guitar, half-sized guitar, three-quarter-sized guitar, full-sized guitar, Grammy.

150

When Elliot died, he became a tree.

Approximately 107 billion people have lived and died

on the planet Earth, and the majority of these souls now live in trees.

Fortunately, there are roughly three trillion trees in the world, so whenever a tree with a soul dies or is cut down, that tree's soul moves into one of the many remaining soulless trees.

Before transitioning from human to tree, people who have led bad lives and committed evil deeds often realise the error of their ways and are truly sorry. These people seek, and usually receive, an absolution and go on to inhabit trees in sociable forests.

However, some souls are truly rotten, and these souls live as lone shrubs in the Arctic tundra.

151

It was 14th July, 2076, and Karen had just turned a hundred years old.

Even though turning a hundred years old wasn't that much of a big deal anymore, the care home staff still liked to make a fuss over their new centenarians; especially when the centenarians were as delightful as Karen.

While Karen's physical agility was poor, her mental agility was as supple as a gymnast, and to all the world she was as cheerful as a summer's day. Yet, privately, she harboured a fear of dying.

Harley, the care assistant who was like the child that Karen had never had, presented Karen with her birthday cards.

After Karen finished opening them, Harley's young daughter, Rosie, proffered Karen her laptop. "Would you like to use my computer to check your Friends Connect page, Karen, to see if anyone has sent you a birthday message?"

Not wanting to quash Rosie's enthusiasm, Karen took

the laptop and logged on to the social media site.

Karen had 134 Friends Connect connections, but all of these connections' pages were now just digital legacies of lives once lived, so Karen knew that there wouldn't be any messages waiting for her. It was, therefore, with some surprise that she saw the flashing envelope.

"You have a message, Karen!" squealed Rosie excitedly, seeing the flickering icon.

Karen clicked on the envelope and read the post.

Dearest Karen, Congratulations on your milestone. Enjoy your day and don't be scared, because we will be together again soon. Love, Theo.

"Is Theo a friend of yours?" enthused Rosie.

Karen, who had turned very pale, said, "Yes, Rosie, Theo was a friend of mine. A very special friend."

Theo had been Karen's husband.

152

He'd spent all of his 18 years living in the cottage on the farm. It was all he knew.

They arrived at the railway station and parked the car, and his dad opened the boot and pulled out two large suitcases, each brimming with clothes, shoes and stationery.

He hugged his dad…and then his mum…and then both of them at the same time, and then they sat on the station bench and waited.

Silence.

It was difficult to tell if he was more nervous or excited because the two emotions were so closely entwined.

The train pulled up, and he boarded it while waving goodbye to his parents and his comfort zone. He then looked out of the window and watched as the only county that he'd ever known faded away.

He woke with a jolt when the man on the tannoy system

announced that they would be arriving at their final destination in a couple of minutes' time.

He looked out of the window.

Darkness – yet lights.

People – masses of them.

A patterned, incandescent snake of vehicles – a night-time jam.

It was all so different to what he was used to.

He felt alive.

He felt expectant.

153

It had taken months to save for it, but as she jumped out of the boat and onto the beach, she knew that it had all been worth it because the island was idyllic. She felt a deep sense of joy.

As the wallpaper strip got bigger and bigger, she felt a deep sense of joy.

* * * * *

It had taken three years of intense study, but as he took the scroll and officially qualified, he felt a real sense of satisfaction.

His sock drawer had been a real mess, but after two hours of sorting and tidying, it was neat and ordered, and he felt a real sense of satisfaction.

* * * * *

The wedding had required a lot of hard work and planning, but as they stood facing each other, they knew that it had all been worth it, and they felt an intense bond of togetherness.

They managed to get the injured bird back on its feet, and as it flew off, they felt an intense bond of togetherness.

* * * * *

She jumped out of the plane and felt a rush of adrenaline. This was pure excitement.

The hay sprang up into the air and danced around in an animated frenzy.

She'd never seen a dust devil before, so this was pure excitement.

154

"Of all the numbers, only 'four' comprises the same number of letters as its number," said Chai.

The cogs in Grandpa Robert's brain started whirring. *One – three; two – three; three – five; four – four; five – four...*

155

They moved into the fast lane and were tailgated by a sports car driver whose music was louder than a howler monkey family wedding. As they tucked back into the slow lane, the sports car driver whizzed past them, displaying one of the digits on his left hand.

"How lovely," said Joanna to her husband, Dave. "What a delightful human being."

She hoped that their three-year-old daughter, who was sitting in the back of the car, hadn't seen the driver's rude gesture.

A few minutes later, they came to a roundabout and pulled up alongside the sports car driver, whose music was now so loud it would have drowned out a foghorn connected to a series of amplifiers.

Joanna started fiddling around with her phone, and the sports car driver's hardcore techno music suddenly transitioned into a stentorian rendition of 'Row Row Row Your Boat'. The driver looked embarrassed and frantically tried to turn the music off.

As Dave and Joanna exited the roundabout, Joanna turned off her phone's Bluetooth.

156

It was Patrick's first time as a best man, and he wasn't going to lie; he was nervous. He wanted the day to go as swimmingly as possible for both his best friend and his best friend's wife-to-be.

A few hours into the wedding, it was time for the speeches, and after hilarious performances from both the bride's father and the groom, Patrick knew that the pressure was on.

He stood up and took the microphone.

"Well, ladies and gentleman, I think we can all agree that it's been a very emotional day so far, as even the cake's in tiers."

Laughter.

Phew.

He had *hilariousbestmanlines.com* to thank for that.

"I first met Ted when I had no money, slept all the time and lived on junk food. And, no, ladies and gentleman, I don't mean when I was a student."

Laughter again.

Brilliant.

But when Patrick caught Ted's eye, they both knew what Patrick had meant. Patrick had first met Ted when Patrick was homeless and living on the streets.

"When I first met Ted, he showed me some kindness, and that kindness really resonated with me, so I resolved to get my life back together and one day help others like Ted had helped me."

The wedding guests all 'ahhed', although some were expecting a punchline.

But there wasn't one.

It was after Ted had thrown some coins into Patrick's jar and given Patrick his packed lunch that Patrick had had his epiphany. Ted's kindness had made Patrick realise that there *was* good in the world and it *was* worth giving life a second shot, so he went back to his family home and made his peace, then he got a part-time job and enrolled at college. A few years later, he qualified as a paramedic.

"Now let's talk about Ted's hobbies," said Patrick, loosening up. "Did you know that Ted once tried to ride a unicycle? And did you know that, while attempting to master his one-wheeled bike, he saw a pretty girl, pedalled as fast as he could and ended up flat on his face? Now, you'd have thought, ladies and gentlemen, that this would have stopped young Ted in his romantic tracks – but, no.

The collapsed heap that was our groom here, dusted down his clothes, smoothed his hair and drew himself to his full height, then he plucked a dandelion from the side of the path and asked the bewildered girl if she'd go on a date with him.

The guests howled.

"However, there's more!" continued Patrick, animatedly. "The young girl, Annabel, said 'yes'…and here we all are today!"

Ted laughed, thinking back to his comedy crash. He then thought back to his not-so-comedy crash, when he'd very nearly lost his life. However, he hadn't lost his life, as Patrick had turned up and saved him.

"And Ted's sporting prowess doesn't stop there, ladies and gentlemen," continued Patrick. "Just last year, Ted decided to run the Leeds marathon, and he trained hard, hoping to complete it in four hours. And he *did* complete it in four hours, ladies and gentleman – he completed it in four hours and 130 minutes."

More howling.

"But, now, in all seriousness, Ted is one of the kindest, most amazing human beings I've ever met. So, ladies and gentleman, can we all now stand and raise our glasses to Ted and his lovely wife, Annabel – to Ted and Annabel!"

"To Ted and Annabel!" repeated the guests, raising their glasses.

157

"Did you hear how the humans have copied us?" said Mrs Kingfisher to Mr Kingfisher.

"No, do tell."

"They realised that the shape of our beaks enables us to dive into water while barely making a splash, so some of their trains have been designed to emulate our beaks, making them faster and quieter."

158

Attractive male: tall, dark, handsome, intelligent, rich, successful, deluded. Seeking Panglossian female.

159

"Do you like the silver bells?" asked the gardener, pointing to the beautiful silver bell snowdrop trees.

"Hate them," spat back Mary, going dewy-eyed, and smiling, at the sight of the charming trees.

She really is contrary, thought the gardener.

160

"I didn't mean to upset your husband," said Sheila, reading out Gracie's text. "What does that mean?"

"What do you mean 'what does that mean'?" said Derek, Sheila's husband. "It seems pretty clear to me. Gracie and Graham didn't mean to upset me and Pete."

Three days earlier, Derek and Sheila, Pete and Jane, and Gracie and Graham had gone on a daytrip – and, during lunch, Gracie and Graham had got into a heated debate with Derek and Pete.

"Well, does it mean that Gracie didn't mean to upset you, but Graham did – '*I* didn't mean to upset your husband'. Gracie did tell Graham to pipe down a few times when he got a bit forthright and aggressive. Or does it mean that Gracie didn't mean to upset you, but she did mean to upset Pete – 'I didn't mean to upset *your* husband'. I mean, Gracie's never really liked Pete, we all know that, so maybe this was her opportunity to lay into him? Or does it mean that Gracie didn't mean to upset you, but she did me, by upsetting you – 'I didn't mean to upset your *husband*'. We all know that she's never really forgiven me for getting the job over her."

"Oh. My. Goodness," said Derek. "There's over-analysing, and then there's over-analysing."

161

"Passions were running high tonight," announced the newsreader as footage of a group of hugging, screaming – and potentially inebriated – fans was shown, "on the day the national team brought home the Junkiter Cup."

<Cue the music>

"Good evening, and welcome to the Six O'Clock News.

"Earlier today, our athletes made sporting history by winning the Junkiter Cup.

"In what turned out to be a nail-biting finale, our women pulled through to win 7-6.

"Tim Scott is with Captain Jill Hinkley now."

"Hi Jill. What a terrific performance today. How did you and your teammates manage to turn things around in the final minute?"

"A pure will to succeed, I think. We were not going to be beaten!"

"And how does it feel to have made sporting history?"

"It hasn't really sunk in yet, to be honest."

"You said before the game that this was going to be your last competitive match. Is that still the plan?"

"Yes. I'm 35 now, so it's definitely time to hang up my boots."

"And what are your plans going forward?"

"Er, I'm not sure yet. For now, I'm just going to enjoy the moment."

"Well, congratulations once again to you and the team – and now it's back to the studio."

* * * * *

She walked into the counsellor's office not knowing whether to bother with any more sessions, as she wasn't sure they were helping.

"How are you doing, Jill? Have you thought any more about what you want to do with the rest of your life?"

Jill glanced up at the wall and saw a photo of her and the team holding the Junkiter Cup.

There had only ever been one thing that she'd wanted to do with her life.

162

There's never a particularly good time for your cooker to give up the ghost, but a particularly bad time is when your house is on the market and it's nearly Christmas. So Keith and Barbara spent their Sunday afternoon oven shopping.

They were out for a bargain because they knew that they wouldn't get much use out of a new cooker due to their imminent move, and their perseverance paid off, as they found a store that was selling the oven they wanted for £50 less than all the other stores.

They drove home feeling smug.

Later that day, the estate agent called to say that Keith and Barbara's offer on the house they wanted had been rejected, but the vendor would take it off the market right away if they'd be willing to pay £660,000.

After a frantic few seconds of whispered discussion, they agreed, even though they hadn't wanted to pay more than £620,000.

She was being followed.

Of that she was sure.

The streets weren't dead, but they weren't bustling either, and the light was beginning to fade.

Instead of heading to her flat, which she reasoned would be a stupid thing to do because she didn't want her pursuer to know where she lived, she was taking a random route. She was choosing the streets that were the most lit up and contained the most people, and she was cursing that she'd left her mobile phone at work.

She saw a coffee shop and walked in, not knowing if her pursuer had followed her, as she was too scared to turn around.

She joined the drinks queue and sensed people filing up behind her.

She ordered a skinny latte and was asked her name so lied and said 'Jane', then watched as the barista scribbled the false moniker onto the side of her cup.

She progressed to the second counter to pay, and when the second barista handed her the card machine, she made sure that he could see her type 9-9-9.

"Jane," bellowed the second barista. "It's been so long I didn't recognise you there for a minute. It's me – Ollie. Ollie Collins. We used to go to school together."

"Oh, yes – Ollie," responded 'Jane'. "I didn't recognise you, either. How are you?"

"You can manage on you own for a while, can't you, Rich" said Ollie, turning to the surprised-looking first barista, "while I spend a few minutes catching up with Jane?"

Ollie ushered 'Jane' up the stairs at the back of the coffee shop, and once she was in the coffee shop staff room, her words tumbled out like rocks in a landslide.

"My name's Beth Hallington.

"Someone's been following me.

"For the past half hour.

"Call the Police.

"Help me.

"I'm so scared."

"Don't worry," said the quick-thinking second barista. "You're safe now."

164

"What a tool," laughed Gavin, showing Phil a picture of the Chief Executive, Dai Pillinger, holding up a sign saying 'McHake's cars McHake you happy'.

"Yes," agreed Phil. "How do these people get to the top?"

"Have you seen his latest blog as well? Talks about what he got up to on his holidays, which is really insensitive given we're all currently maxed out trying to get the Mc3 designs ready."

"Moron," agreed Phil.

The following week, Gavin was walking down the corridor at exactly the same time Dai Pillinger was walking up the corridor.

"Hello Gavin," said Dai.

Gavin was astonished that Dai knew his name. "Er...hello Dai."

"Tell me, Gavin, what do you and your colleagues think of my blogs? Find them useful?"

"Er, yes, Dai, they're very...er...informative." Gavin sensed that Dai was enjoying watching him squirm.

"Oh, good, I *am* pleased to hear you say that."

When Gavin got back to his desk, he told Phil about his encounter, and Phil fell off his chair laughing.

A couple of weeks later, Phil was hard at work

designing the Mc3's pillar trim, and in desperate need of a distraction, he checked out the latest entry in Dai Pillinger's blog, 'I spy with my little eye'.

On reading the entry, Phil learnt about Dai's weekend playing 'I spy' with his 11-year-old niece.

"Who cares what Pillinger was doing at the weekend?" he grumbled, showing Gavin the blog.

"Yeah," agreed Gavin. "What an idiot."

That afternoon, Phil was in the kitchen making the coffees when Dai suddenly appeared.

"Good weekend?" asked Dai.

"Er, yes, thanks," said Phil, suddenly discovering he could make coffee very quickly.

"I spent the weekend with my little niece, Greta. Fun, kids, aren't they?"

"Yes, fun," said Phil, before snatching his tray of drinks and rushing back to his office.

"There's something funny going on," he said as he got back to his desk and gave Gavin a half-filled cup of coffee with neither coffee nor milk in it.

He then scrutinised his new laptop and spotted the covert webcam.

165

Kerry, Bill, Will and Molly were a close-knit family of four who were forced to work the fields every day.

The Kathrokas demanded that the family start at four a.m. and finish at nine p.m., and if the Kathrokas felt that their humans weren't pulling their weight, they'd beat them; a painful punishment given the Kathrokas' great height and weight advantage.

Molly was nearly 14 years old, and the Kathrokas deemed her healthy and strong, so she was chosen for the breeding programme.

Two months before Molly was due to leave for the programme, her mum, Kerry, sprained her wrist while out in the fields.

The family knew that this was 'game over'.

When the Kathrokas realised that Kerry was no longer an effective worker, they enrolled her on the advanced feeding programme.

On the day that Molly was sent away to the breeding chambers, the Kathroka family tucked into their roast Kerry sandwiches.

166

I'm the colour of blood.

My neighbour shares her name with a fruit.

Her neighbour is the colour of the sun.

His neighbour is the colour of grass.

My neighbour's, neighbour's, neighbour's neighbour is the colour of the sky.

Her neighbour has a much deeper, and darker, colour.

His neighbour shares her name with a flower.

Then it stopped raining, and we were gone.

167

He liked to tease his students. One time, Maisie's phone went off in the middle of his lecture, so he grabbed the pulsating device, answered it and agreed that Maisie would go salsa dancing with Suzie that evening. Another time, he pretended that there was going to be an impromptu exam, but when his students turned their test papers over, the papers read, 'Only joking!'

Despite – or perhaps because of – his teasing, Dr

Collinson was one of the most popular lecturers at the university.

* * * * *

As one particular lecture came to an end, Dr Collinson told his students that they'd need to put their thinking caps on in his next lecture because he'd be teaching them about general relativity, which was hard to get your head around.

That evening, Maisie was on social media.

Suzie: *How was your day?*

Maisie: *Yeah, okay, thanks. Yours?*

Suzie: *Alright, although I have an assignment due in tomorrow and haven't even started it!*

Maisie: *Nightmare. Going to be a late one?*

Suzie: *Yep. How's your funny lecturer? The one I spoke to about the salsa class?!*

Maisie: *Still a wind-up merchant! He says that our next lecture's going to be really hard, and we'll need to put our thinking caps on.*

Suzie: *You should all turn up in hats!*

Maisie: *Yeah, good one! Right, I'm going to forbid you to chat to me anymore, Suzie, else you'll be up all night doing your assignment.*

Suzie: *Yes mum!*

Maisie: *Ha! See you tomorrow night at salsa...which I hate!*

After messaging Suzie, Maisie kept thinking about her friend's idea, and after a couple of hours of umming and ahing, she finally bit the bullet and sent a message to the physics group. She didn't know what sort of a response she'd get, though, as a lot of the other students seemed very serious-minded.

But she was pleasantly surprised...

* * * * *

"Good morning, reprobates," said Dr Collinson, striding into the lecture theatre. "And it's a miracle to see so many of you at a morning lecture. Has the student nightclub closed down?"

The students rolled their eyes.

"So, today, as promised, we're going to be learning about general relativity." Dr Collinson turned to the whiteboard and started writing. "In Walter Isaacson's biography of Albert Einstein, Isaacson defines the theory of relativity as follows." Dr Collinson turned round to his students and said, "And now's the time to put your thinking caps on, as this is seriously confusing."

As Dr Collinson turned back round to face the whiteboard, Maisie stood up and gave her classmates a big thumbs-up, and they all put on their hats.

"Isaacson says that the general theory of relativity can be described using a thought experiment. Picture what it would be like to roll a bowling ball onto the two-dimensional surface of a trampoline, and then roll on some billiard balls. The billiard balls would move towards the bowling ball because the bowling ball would curve the trampoline fabric.

"Now imagine this happening in the four-dimensional fabric of space and time.

"Does any of this make any sense?"

As Dr Collinson posed the question, he turned round and saw the sea of hats.

"Excellent!" he giggled. "Excellent! Thinking caps, right?!"

He kept laughing.

"Touché," he concluded. "Touché!"

168

"Leaving early again, Han?" sneered Chris as Han packed up her things and left the office. "Part-timer," he muttered under his breath.

As Han made her way out of the office, she looked over at her manager, Rose, who raised her eyebrows in an apologetic way. Rose wanted to defend Han but understood why Han wanted to keep her private life private.

After getting into her car, which was parked in the company car park, Han drove to the hospital for her latest round of treatment.

169

"What a good boy am I!"

"No, you're really not," grumbled Jack's teacher, cross that Jack had a plum skewered to his thumb. "Go and sit on the naughty step."

Little Jack Horner picked up his Christmas pie and went and sat on the seat of shame in the corner of the classroom. Once there, he found a second plum in his pie, which he skewered onto his other thumb. "What a good boy am I!" he said again.

"No, you're really not," repeated Jack's teacher, who hated teaching at the nursery school and wondered what alternative careers he could pursue. However, he was soon distracted when Little Miss Muffet let out a yelp of joy on seeing a spider.

The technical plan was due in by close of play, so he knew he needed to knuckle down and really get going with it.

I'll just go and get a cup of water from the machine to ensure I'm well-hydrated, he thought.

On returning to his desk with his water, he checked his mobile phone to see if the garage had rung about his car. There were no missed calls, but as he had his phone in his hand, he thought he'd just quickly scroll through his social media accounts to see if anyone had posted anything interesting.

Ten minutes later, he laid down his phone and unlocked his computer screen.

There was a sudden loud 'thud' from the corner of the office, and he looked up to see his colleague, Emma, showing his other colleague, Raj, how to juggle. They were using apples.

I know how to juggle, he thought, bounding over to demonstrate.

Circus act over, he returned to his desk and sat in his chair.

I'm sure that this chair could be better set up for me, he thought, fiddling around with the various screws, levers and bulbs.

"Right, the plan," he said to himself, after achieving the perfect chair configuration. "I'll just pop to the loo first."

On his way back from the toilet, he bumped into Debbie and asked how her karate lessons were going.

Back at his desk, he was about to start writing the first paragraph of his plan when his friend Nikki turned up and asked if he fancied joining her for lunch.

An hour later, he returned to his desk and checked the company intranet, which featured an update on the new rail-booking system. Even though he never travelled anywhere with his job, he thought it important to properly read it.

Having read the article, and thinking that he really must now focus, he heard a groan to his left and saw Annabel carrying, and almost dropping, a tray of hot drinks. He rushed over to her and opened all of the doors that she needed to go through.

Back at his desk, he added a few more rubber bands to the rubber band ball he was making, then he grabbed his mug and ambled over to the kitchen to make himself a cup of coffee. There was a pile of unwashed mugs in the kitchen, so he washed them all up.

He returned to his desk and became embroiled in a debate about the relative merits of the parsnip versus the carrot. Debate over – the parsnip won – he looked at his watch and took a sharp intake of breath.

It was four p.m.

Rats.

Over the next hour, his fingers moved at ferocious speed, and a nearby colleague was convinced she could see steam coming out of them.

At five p.m. on the dot, he emailed his completed plan to his boss, then got up and left the office for the day.

171

"If you could each stand up and explain why you're here, that'd be brilliant," grinned the therapist.

"I used my cunning and wiliness to drive a man to kill his wife," said the first man.

"I'm a psychotic murderer," said the second.

"I seduce my victims, then fatally bite them," announced the third.

"Some say that I'm crime personified," shared the fourth.

"I murdered my girlfriend in a brutal way," declared the fifth.

"And I took away Christmas," said the only woman and the final member of the group.

"Good, good," enthused the therapist. "The first step to becoming a better person is to understand where you went wrong in the past, so that was great."

Iago, Hannibal, Dracula, Moriarty, Bill Sikes and the White Witch all looked at each other, bemused.

172

I was washed up onto the beach, barely conscious.

A man and a woman ran over to me, and the woman tapped three digits into her phone while the man threw water over me, being careful to avoid my blowhole.

173

A snail.

That was his tag.

That was the way to tell that it was his work.

My best friend had been a thatcher for over twenty years, and he'd had clients across the whole of the country, such was his excellent reputation. His material of choice had been water reed, as he'd said that water reed lasts longer than wheat and straw.

When he emigrated, he left a hole. Not in any of his roofs, as he was too good a thatcher for that, but in my life.

A few days after he left, his sister suggested that we go on a road trip to cheer ourselves up, and after much persuasion, I agreed.

As we travelled the length and breadth of the country,

passing through the picturesque towns and villages, I realised that his presence was everywhere.

How I loved to see those water reed snails.

174

"Nose in a medical book again, boy? Go and find yourself a respectable trade."

At 14 years old, Eddie was very impressionable, so the gruff postmaster's words really made him question his passions and interests.

* * * * *

It's thought that Edward Jenner's pioneering work in immunology saved more than 530 million lives.

175

Felix grabbed the shears from out of the shed, walked over to the yew tree and started chopping.

A couple of hours later, he stood back from his masterpiece and baulked. *A heart? This was more like an anatomical one.*

"Don't panic," he said to himself. "You'll just have to try again and create a smaller one."

An hour or so later, he stepped back from his second attempt and baulked again.

This pattern continued until there were hardly any yew tree leaves left.

"What have I done?" he squeaked.

* * * * *

Felix sat in the lounge, nervously awaiting Lydia's return. On hearing the car pull up on the drive, he rushed to the front door, opened it and shouted "Happy Anniversary" while thrusting a bouquet of flowers into his wife's face.

Lydia could smell a rat straight away, as you didn't get to forty years of marriage without knowing when your partner was up to no good.

"What have you done, Felix?" she asked suspiciously.

"What do you mean?" squeaked Felix, feigning innocence.

Lydia barged down the hallway and burst into the kitchen.

Everything seemed to be okay.

She then looked out of the window and gasped.

"My yew tree! My lovely yew tree!"

"I'm so sorry, Lyds," whimpered Felix. "I tried to shape it into a heart for you, but it didn't quite turn out as planned."

Lydia looked at Felix sternly.

Then her face softened.

Unlike the yew tree, Felix had a big heart.

176

"Did you hear how the humans have copied us?" said Mrs Butterfly to Mr Butterfly.

"No, do tell."

"They studied the way that our wings gleam in bright light, and they've used this information to develop colour displays for their e-readers that enable them to read in sunlight.

177

I got a really bad virus, which I didn't want to pass on to others, but I couldn't stop them from opening up their emails.

178

Choosing what colour car to have was the first big decision I had to make – I chose green.

I then had to decide whether to further my studies or go into business – I chose the university route.

I got married early on in my life – it was forced upon me.

Then I was pegged down with children.

And life wasn't plain sailing after having children – I broke my neck in a car crash and had a midlife crisis.

Apparently, the winner of 'The Game of Life' was the person who earned the most money, but even from a young age, I wasn't sure that was true.

179

"I'm going to school! I'm going to school!" he sang in eager anticipation. And his uniform. My word his uniform. How proud was he of that?

Five-year-old Henry couldn't sleep the night before his first day at school, such was his excitement at the thought of becoming a schoolboy.

* * * * *

"I don't want to go to school!" he screamed, slamming the door and skulking off.

Fifteen-year-old Henry couldn't sleep the night before his first day back at high school, such was his dread at having to spend yet another year at the heinous place. And how he hated having to wear a uniform. He felt that it was further evidence of the teachers trying to turn him into a mindless, homogenous clone.

180

So many freckles. How had he ended up with so many freckles?

As an eight-year-old, he'd decided to take matters into his own hands, so one afternoon he shut himself in the family bathroom and started to systematically scrape off the offending spots, beginning with his left arm. He used the opened scissor blade, and after an hour or two of scraping, was left with a very bloodied and painful arm. When his mother – who'd been wondering where he was – walked into the bathroom and saw the spectacle, she sank onto the floor in horror. What had he done?

That evening, after an afternoon at A&E getting his arm stitched and dressed, his parents sat him down and asked him why he'd done what he'd done, and he told them that the boy in the year above him had called him a dot-to-dot, which he hadn't liked. His parents said that, unfortunately, children often said and did horrible things to each other, but this would stop when he and the other children got older. They also said that there was nothing wrong with having freckles. They said that freckles made people look more interesting – just like Tiddles, their cat, looked more interesting thanks to his handsome tortoiseshell markings.

At 28, he thought back to that conversation and realised that his parents hadn't been entirely truthful with him, as some adults also said and did horrible things to each other.

The gunman had rounded him and the other customers up, so he was currently sitting on the floor in the middle of the café, wondering if this was going to be his last day on Earth.

As the hours passed, he tried to to remain calm by thinking back to the key chapters of his life – his school years; his student years; his career; his wedding; the travelling he'd done; the people he'd met along the way. However, when he could no longer block out his fear with his memories, he started fidgeting, and he felt the scars on his left arm and wondered what he'd been thinking that day in the bathroom.

He began joining up the damaged, freckly dots.

He scored a fish...then a car...then a rhombus...then a pan.

As a female customer who'd asked to go to the toilet returned from the facilities, shaking, the terrorist traced her every move with his gun.

A sudden flurry of activity.

A crash.

A yelp.

A pool of blood.

A pan by the fallen terrorist's head.

181

As the fastest man in the world that year and the 100-metre world record holder, he hoped he had a decent chance of getting through to the final.

The gun fired.

He exploded out of the blocks, keeping his body forward and his head down.

At 50 metres, his head was up and he was running tall, picking up his knees and holding his shoulders down. He was now at full speed.

At 80 metres, he glanced to his right…then to his left…and he knew he wasn't going to do it.

Only the four fastest athletes from each semi-final would go through to the final, and the cheetah, pronghorn, springbok and hare were all well ahead of him.

182

"I hate Norma," said Ben. "She's ruined my life."

"We all thought that she'd cause a lot of damage, and sadly she did," sighed Rosie.

"A lot of damage is an understatement," said Ben. "She's a home-wrecker."

"She is," agreed Rosie, stroking Ben's arm. "I hear that she killed a few people, too?"

"Yes," said Ben. "Six, I think."

"So sad," said Rosie, thinking about the victims of the hurricane.

183

"Right then, Ethel, are you ready for the toilet?" asked the carer.

"I am," whispered Ethel, bracing herself for the indignity ahead.

The lavatorial ordeal over, Ethel returned to the lounge to sit with all the other old people. Ethel didn't say much, but she thought a lot. She'd often just sit in her chair knitting; her mind racing.

That particular afternoon, Percy had a guest, which rarely happened because Percy didn't have many friends left, and his only child had emigrated from the UK to

Australia. However, Percy's grandson, Julian, was back from Australia for a couple of weeks, and he was keen to catch up with his beloved grandfather.

"Hello grandpa, how are you?" enthused Julian, bouncing into the lounge.

Unfortunately, Percy's speaking abilities had really deteriorated over the past few months, so Julian didn't get much of a response out of his grandpa – just a small smile of recognition.

"It's nice to be back in the UK," persisted Julian, not really knowing what to do other than continue with his chatter, "and I had a good flight over here, grandpa – I managed to sleep for a bit of it."

The carer walked over to Julian and gave him a cup of tea, and he smiled at her while running his fingers over the bulging veins on his grandfather's hand.

"The Formula One's been interesting this season, grandpa, although Ryder Fascar is dominating again." As Julian said this, he sensed a sharp movement to his right, and he turned to see an old lady staring at him.

"I'm Julian," said Julian, nodding at the lady. "Do you like motor racing, too?"

"I'm Ethel," replied the lady.

"Ethel's more of a knitter than a motor racer, aren't you, Ethel?" joked the carer.

"In World War Two, I was part of the team that fitted R.A.E. restrictors in Merlin engines," said Ethel. "I mostly worked on Spitfires."

As Julian's interest visibly piqued, the carer's jaw visibly dropped, as she'd never heard Ethel say more than a few words before.

"Did you work for Beatrice Shilling, Ethel?" asked Julian, clearly very impressed.

"I did," said Ethel, her eyes lighting up on learning that Julian knew about Beatrice. "After the war, Beatrice and her husband taught me how to ride a motorbike...then how to race a car."

"What did you race?" asked Julian excitedly.

"The Austin-Healey Sebring Sprite was one of my favourites," began Ethel.

Over the next hour, Julian sat listening to Ethel's stories, enraptured. And Percy listened to them, too; equally enraptured.

184

"Don't tie yourself up in knots over it," said Christian, seeing Amber agonising over which yellow spot to put her left hand on.

185

You humans didn't realise that when you said things like 'how nice of him', you were referring to us, not him. *You* were just the carriers.

I wasn't niceness, or evilness, or sadness. I was serendipity. And we each had an opposing force, and mine was zemblanity.

People often talk about the fight between good and evil, and it's a fight that my two brethren currently have – and that their ancestors have had, and that future generations will have. But my fight was with zemblanity. Whereas I was all about pleasant surprises, zemblanity brought about unpleasant unsurprises. So if I wanted there to be more pleasant surprises than unpleasant unsurprises in the world, I had to work harder than my nemesis.

We each had a twenty-year tenure before we were rested and replaced, and during our tenures we would usually balance out, slightly dominate, or be slightly dominated by our opposing forces. However, there had been times when certain forces had completely dominated their nemeses, and this had resulted in hugely positive, or negative, periods in history. Take the Crusades, for example. During those bloody hundreds of years, tolerance's and benevolence's ancestors had utterly failed to keep their opposing forces in check.

186

"Wasn't it enough that I was wooden, Carlo? Did you really have to have the whole nose-growing thing, too?"

"Don't you go blaming me, young man. Blame Geppetto – he made you."

"Don't you bring me into this, Carlo. You made me make Pinocchio. You're the writer."

"Yeah, Carlo. Don't blame dad."

"It's just that the nose-growing thing added an extra dimension to the story, Pinocchio. And it taught young children not to lie."

"But is lying always a bad thing?"

"Well, I think it is."

"Maybe it's sometimes a kindness?"

"No. You shouldn't lie, Pinocchio."

"I'm not lying – do you see a big nose?"

"No, I know you're not lying, Pinocchio. I meant that you shouldn't lie, not that *you* shouldn't lie."

"Huh?"

"Maybe my boy has a point, Carlo?"

"How so, Geppetto?"

"Well, do you like Carlo's striped trousers, Pinocchio?"

"Oh yes, very much," said Pinocchio as his nose started to grow.

"What's wrong with my trousers?" asked Carlo defensively.

187

"She's so lazy."

"Oh course she's lazy; she's a rest. Why do you have to be so sharp?"

"Oh shut up. I'd rather be sharp than flat."

"Ggrr. Hiss. Boo. Leave flat alone. I've had enough of your sharpness."

"I'll say whatever I want to say to flat. Why do you have to be so crotchety?"

"Leeave-crrotchet-aalone."

"Oh stop your slurring."

"Will. You. Be. Nice. Please. Sharp."

Flat, Crotchet, Slur and Staccato knew that they'd never change Sharp. Only Natural could temper Sharp's acerbity.

188

I was thrown from my desk when the – what I assumed to be – earthquake happened. I became very cold, then blacked out and never came round.

* * * * *

Similar to a game of golf, the aim was to use the stick to hit the terrestrial planet or asteroid as far as you could.

Age: 10

Dear diary. I've decided to start a diary so I can read it back and remember what I did with my life from the age of 10. Love Isaac.

Age: 10 and ¼

Dear diary. A baby called Stella was born today, and apparently she's my sister. Stella will be at the hospital with the lady who's my mummy for a few days. Love Isaac.

Age: 10 and ¼

Dear diary. I was told that I have a baby sister called Stella, and Stella's at the hospital with my mummy. Love Isaac.

Age: 10 and ¼

Dear diary. I found out today that I have a little sister called Stella, and Stella's coming home from the hospital tomorrow. Love Isaac.

Age: 10 and ¼

Dear diary. I have a little sister called Stella, and Stella came home today. Stella's small and squidgy, so the people who said that they were my mummy and daddy told me to be very gentle with her. Love Isaac.

Age: 22 and ½

Dear diary. She's called Amelia, and she's perfect. She smiled at me in a bar, so we got chatting, and we bonded like peanut butter and jam. She's coming round to my flat in three days' time, and I think that she could be 'the one'. Isaac.

Age: 22 and ½
Dear diary. A girl called Amelia turned up at my flat today, and I knew that she would because you told me she would. Amelia's amazing, and I agree with myself when I said that she could be 'the one'. Isaac.

Age: 29
Dear diary. Today was my wedding day, and it was really good fun. The speeches were hilarious, and I learnt that I've done some really goofy things in the past. Amelia seems like a really nice person, and she arranged for a videographer to film the wedding for me so I can watch it back and remember it. Isaac.

Age: 35 and ¾
Dear diary. Amelia seems like a really nice person, and when I woke, she gave me a ring-binder filled with notes and photographs explaining who I am. Later in the day, I took her to the hospital, and she gave birth to twins. They're called Joshua and Caroline. Isaac.

Age: 35 and ¾
Dear diary. I didn't sleep very well last night, as there was lots of crying. Amelia, who I'm told is my wife, said that we'd have to get used to not sleeping for a while. Isaac.

Age: 40
Dear diary. Today was my 40th birthday, and when I woke, the lady next to me gave me a ring-binder filled with notes and photos explaining who I am, and who she is. I learnt that I have two children, and those children came running into my bedroom to give me a card and a present. They're very energetic! Isaac.

Age: 40 and one day
Dear diary. I woke up today and knew who I was! I could remember yesterday, when I turned 40 and looked

through the ring-binder. I'm going to see the doctor tomorrow, so here's hoping my memory might be starting to function. Isaac.

Age: 40 and ½
Dear diary. One hundred and eighty days have passed, and I can remember every single one of them! I don't know how Amelia and my family coped all those years when I had to meet them for the first time every day. Long may my memory continue to function! Isaac.

Age: 45
Dear diary. The strangest thing happened today. I could still remember everything from the past five years, but I also had a memory of starting school! In my memory, my parents introduced themselves to me and told me it was my first day at school, then they dressed me in grey shorts and a purple jumper, and then we left the house and walked to the infant school.

I rang my parents to tell them about my memory, and they said that it was correct. I don't know what this means, but we'll see what tomorrow brings. Isaac.

Age: 50 and ¼
Dear diary. Something very exciting happened today – I remembered being told about Stella's birth! Isaac.

Age: 62 and ½
Dear diary. It's been a very busy day today because it's now only three days until Caroline's wedding, so she had us all making favours. Today was also a very special day for me because I remembered meeting Amelia for the first time (as in the first time I actually met her – not any of the subsequent times, when I *thought* I was meeting her for the first time). Amelia smiled at me in a bar, so I went over to her and we got chatting. I told Amelia what I'd remembered, and she got quite emotional. Isaac.

Age: 65

Dear diary. Today I had a memory from when I was 25. I hit a male cyclist while out driving, so I got out of my car, dialled 999 and started doing CPR on the man. The ambulance turned up, and I followed it to the hospital, where I stayed with the comatose cyclist all day. That evening, I was too distressed to write anything in my diary.

Feeling very anxious, I told Amelia about my memory, and when I asked her what had happened to the man, she turned pale and wouldn't tell me. I got very upset because, unless she told me what had happened to the man, I'd never know (because I wouldn't have given it another thought after the day of the accident, as I'd have forgotten it). I have this awful feeling that the man didn't make it, so I'm feeling really guilty right now. Isaac.

Age: 65

Dear diary. Amelia finally told me what happened to the man. He did die, so I did kill him. The guilt is hard to bear, and this is the first time that I wish that I hadn't got my memories back. Isaac.

Age: 80

Dear diary. I've finally got all of my memories back, as I can now remember the first forty years of my life. Isaac.

190

"What's half of seven?"

"Eight is half of seven; seven is half of six; six is half of five; five is half of four; four is half of three; three is half of two; two is half of one; and one is half of nought."

"Very good. A+."

"Is A+ a paper size?"

191

They were excited to be attempting the escape room.

In an escape room, a team was locked in a room, and the players had to use elements of the room to solve a series of clues and puzzles in order to escape from the room within a set time limit.

There were four of them, and they had exactly one hour to escape from this particular room.

They entered the room, and the countdown began: 60:00, 59:59, 59:58…

There was a table in the middle of the room, and on top of the table was a loaf of bread, a red plastic fish, a basket and a drawing board.

They looked around the rest of the room, which was very kitchen-like, and Sally discovered a note propped up on a shelf, instructing them to 'add 64 to 20, divide by 2, deduct 30, and divide by 4'.

"Let's use the easel to figure it out!" she shouted.

That one didn't work, thought Nick, the game designer. Nick was watching the four players on the CCTV and liked to play his own little game while they played theirs. *0-1 to them.*

The team congregated around the drawing board and used the pen and paper to work out the answer to the sum.

"Hhmm…what's the significance of three?" pondered Peter as Jane spotted a cake. The cake was cut into eight pieces, and each piece had a number iced on top.

"It's a piece of cake!" shouted Jane.

1-1, thought Nick.

Sally, Peter and Hugh turned to look at Jane, who'd taken the piece of cake with the three on top and crumbled it up to find a key. She then used that key to unlock the fridge, which contained some milk, four eggs and a jar of fake maggots.

48:42, 48:41, 48:40…

Back at the table, Hugh discovered some writing on the bottom of the basket – *Fill the basket to reveal the next clue, but don't go ova.* "Guys, I think we need to fill the basket with the eggs to get the next clue!"

Jane and Sally grabbed the eggs from out of the fridge, and they were about to put them in the basket when Hugh suddenly cautioned, "Don't put all the eggs into the basket!"

Hhmm – nearly, thought Nick. *1-2 to them.*

Hugh took the eggs from Jane and Sally and put one in the basket and waited.

Nothing.

He then placed a second egg in the basket and waited.

Nothing.

However, when he placed a third egg in the basket, a piece of paper appeared under the door that they'd used to enter the room.

Peter grabbed the piece of paper and was confused to see that it was blank.

"Maybe there's invisible ink on it?" said Jane, thinking back to her childhood. "If we sprinkle some water on it, a message might appear?"

The team hunted for water, but there was none to be found.

"This room literally contains everything but the kitchen sink," observed Sally, lamenting the lack of a tap.

That one wasn't even planned! thought Nick, triumphantly. *2-2.*

"We could try using the milk?" suggested Jane, spilling a couple of drops of milk onto the paper, but to no avail.

"Don't worry, Jane," said Hugh. "It was worth a try."

Aren't you going to cry over spilled milk? willed Nick. *No, clearly not. 2-3.*

The team was foxed.

And time was ticking.

21:20, 21:19, 21:18…

"Oh boy. What are we meant to do now?" moaned Peter in frustration.

"Use your loaf," piped up a voice – Nick's voice – over the tannoy system.

"We're trying!" shouted back Peter, thinking what an unhelpful piece of advice that was.

"No, he means use *our loaf*," said Sally excitedly.

Hugh caught on at exactly the same time as Sally, and the two of them made a beeline for the loaf of bread on the table, which they crumbled up to reveal a vial of water. They poured the water onto the paper, and some writing appeared.

Explore the cutlery drawer to find what you're looking for.

They rummaged through the utensils and eventually found a key buried amongst all of the forks.

"Are there any locks that we can open with this key?" shouted Sally, and the four of them raced around the room looking for a lock…but to no avail.

14:30, 14:29, 14:28…

"We've searched everywhere," panted Hugh. "There aren't any locks in this room."

Jane started to pull cookbooks off a shelf.

"What are you doing?" chastised Peter. "We're searching for a lock, not a book, Jane!"

Jane opened three of the books, but they were just standard cookbooks. However, when she opened a fourth, there was a locked box inside. "See!" she shouted, showing Peter the box. "Don't judge a book by its cover!"

Oh yes! thought Nick, thoroughly enjoying his private game of idioms. *That was perfect. 3-3.*

9:58, 9:57, 9:56…

Jane unlocked the box, which contained four drinking straws, and one of the drinking straws had a note curled up inside of it. She unfurled the note and read out its contents. "To find the combination to secure your escape, study the animals in the landscape."

"What does that mean?" asked Peter.

"Let's scour the room to see what objects we have left," suggested Sally.

Peter ran over to the fridge and grabbed the jar of maggots, but Hugh said that maybe the maggots were a ruse and maybe the game designer had literally wanted them to 'take the bait'. As he said this, he looked up at the CCTV camera and arched his left eyebrow.

4-3, thought Nick, wondering if Hugh was onto him.

Meanwhile, Sally was standing by the table trying to see if there was anything on the red plastic fish that could maybe help them out. However, Hugh said that this could be a ruse too, and maybe something of a red herring.

5-3. He's definitely onto me.

4:41, 4:40, 4:39…

Peter studied the door, which he presumed would lead to their escape. It had a numerical keypad on it, and he wondered how they were meant to figure out the combination to get out. His gaze drifted to the right…and he saw a painting hanging up on the wall.

A landscape.

"The picture!" he cried.

The team members rushed over to the painting, which featured two sheep; one of which had the number 145 painted on its rump; the other, 32.

1:01, 1:00, 0:59…

Sally ran to the keypad and punched in 14532.

Nothing.

0:33, 0:32, 0:31…

She then tried 32145, and the door opened.

The team members were greeted by Nick, who congratulated them on escaping from the room and asked if they'd enjoyed the game.

"We did, thanks," said Hugh. "Did you enjoy *your* game?"

192

"You could be making history right now. This could be a world first," said Chai as his grandpa shuffled the pack of cards in preparation for their next game of snap.

"Go on, lad," said Grandpa Roberts, wondering what was coming next, knowing his grandson as he did.

"There are more ways to arrange a deck of cards than there are atoms on Earth."

193

Human beings like to explain things away with science, and there have been a number of different explanations for me – Will. One explanation is that I'm the oxidation of phosphine, diphosphane and methane. Do you follow? Me neither. Another is that I'm the bioluminescence of micro-organisms and insects. I struggle to even say bioluminescence, let alone know what it means.

While I applaud the humans' fancy theories, I'm actually just Will-o'-wisp, the naughty, young, water-loving imp who likes to confuse night-time travellers by shining a torch above my head.

194

I didn't usually spend much money on things, but when I saw the limited-edition car, I felt compelled to buy it.

That evening, I visited my mum and dad to show them my shiny new purchase. I say my 'mum and dad', and they were my mum and dad, just not my biological mum and dad...

I'd been left in a box outside mum and dad's local hospital when I was just a few days old, but by happy coincidence, mum and dad had been looking to adopt a baby at that very same time.

Mum and dad loved the car, although they were surprised that I'd splashed out on a new one, as I usually bought cars that were a couple of years old and had depreciated in price. I told them that I didn't know what had come over me, I just knew I had to have it.

A few weeks later, I received a letter in the post saying that I needed to return my car because there was an issue with the limited-edition cars' airbags. I was told to return the car at a particular time, on a particular day, and at a particular location, which I thought was a bit cheeky given the issue was due to manufacturer – rather than driver – error.

At the specified time and date, I turned up at the requested location and parked my car in a car park containing what must have been a hundred other cars just like mine.

As I got out of my car, I saw someone else getting out of their identical car, and as they turned to lock their door, they looked over at me.

And froze.

They were me.

195

"Where shall we start?" asked the vet. "The black horse, the three-legged mare or the swan?"

"Let's have a pint in the Three-legged Mare first," said the vet's best friend.

196

I started having my five-a-day, but I don't mean fruit and veg.

Coming face-to-face with death makes you realise just how mortal you are, and if you're fortunate to survive, you endeavour to cram as much as possible into your remaining years. So I committed to having five new experiences a day – my five-a-day. These experiences didn't have to be high-adrenaline activities – little things, such as taking a different route to work, would count.

Take yesterday, for example. I set my alarm to go off at six a.m. so I could sit in my back garden and watch the sun rise. And, as the day dawned, I sat in my deckchair, listening to the birdsong and watching the squirrels' nimble-footed, death-defying acrobatics.

A couple of hours later, I got into my car and drove to work, spending the commute listening to a genre of music that I wouldn't normally listen to. I'm not sure that I particularly liked the music, but it was good to try something new.

Two things ticked off the day's bucket list, I arrived at work and prepared to tick off the third.

"The thing is, Spike, you emanate negativity like a skunk emanates sulphur, and you collect the plaudits for other people's work like a magpie collects shiny trinkets."

Ah, that felt good. I'd always wanted to say that to the grumpy old curmudgeon, and now, finally, I had.

Later that day, after getting home from work, I made dinner – cooking something I'd never cooked before – and, after swallowing the last, tasty mouthful, I mentally crossed the fourth item off my day's bucket list, then raced outside and got into my car.

As I arrived at the wing-walking centre, I felt the excitement bubbling up in the pit of my stomach like magma in the throat of a volcano.

* * * * *

Unfortunately, yesterday's five-a-day was my last five-a-day on Earth, and I'm regaling you this story from the next life.

As I drove back from the wing-walking centre after one of the most amazing experiences of my life, the teenage driver hit me head-on, and I never stood a chance.

197

I loved my dad, but there were three things that really annoyed me about him.

Firstly, he would always speak for me. I wish he wouldn't do that; I had my own mind and my own voice.

Secondly, he could be very controlling, always making me do what he wanted me to.

And, thirdly, when he'd finished controlling me, he would lock me up in a dark, dingy box.

I bet Sooty wasn't put in a box.

198

"Let's record your heights on the wall before we paper over it," said Mrs Huber. "You first, Abby."

Abby stood with her back to the wall, and Mrs Huber grabbed a pencil, drew a line at the top of Abby's head and wrote, 'Abby, aged 12' next to it.

"Now you, Jakob."

Jakob stood next to the wall, and his mother drew a line above his head and wrote, 'Jakob, aged four' next to it.

"And, last but not least – you, Julia."

Mrs Huber positioned her younger child, Julia, against the wall, then drew a line above her head and scribbled, 'Julia, aged two' next to it.

"Let's do you, too!" enthused Abby. "Jakob, grab the pencil and jump onto my back."

Jakob snatched the pencil from out of his mother's hand while Abby gave him a piggy-back, and he drew a line just above his mother's head and wrote, 'Mummy, aged old' next to it.

"Let's now pop this first piece on," said Mrs Huber, grabbing a sheet of wallpaper and hurriedly papering over Abby's name.

* * * * *

A lot of people attended the funeral, as Mrs Huber had been a well-loved member of the community.

Mrs Huber had also been a well-loved mother, so Jakob and Julia found the service tough but somehow managed to get through it.

A few weeks later, Jakob and Julia finally felt ready to clear out their late mother's house, and after emptying it, they decided to freshen it up a bit by pulling off the old-fashioned wallpaper.

After a couple of hours of hard graft, they were starting to flag, and Jakob was about to take a break when he spotted a line with the words, 'Jakob, aged four' next to it. "Look at this, Jules," he said. "We must have marked our heights on the wall when we were kids."

"Ooh, where am I?" said Julia, tearing down the neighbouring strip of paper. "Oh, here I am!" she squealed, gesturing towards a line near the bottom of the wall.

"And this must be mother," said Jakob, spotting a line about a metre above his own. "Hang on, though, it says Abby. Who's Abby?"

"I've no idea, as mother's line's here," said Julia,

pointing to a line labelled, 'Mummy, aged old'.

* * * * *

"We saw our lines, and then we saw a line with the name 'Abby' pencilled next to it," said Jakob to his elderly auntie.

"So we can only assume that we had an older sister," continued Julia, "and something happened to her?"

"Abby wasn't your sister," said Aunt Ada. "She was Jewish."

Jakob and Julia looked confused...then Julia let out a sudden 'oh'. "Mother hid her when the Germans invaded Holland, didn't she?"

"She did," said Ada.

"So, what happened to her?" asked Jakob, wondering if Abby was still alive and thinking that his mother had been a most remarkable human being.

"She moved on," whispered Ada, thinking it would break his heart to know that he had been the one to let the 'friendly' German officer in on their 'special secret'. Fortunately, the German officer had carried a torch for her sister, otherwise she would have 'moved on', too.

199

"Did you hear how the humans have copied us?" said Mr Shark to Mrs Shark.

"No, do tell."

"They realised that our skin is covered in denticles that overlap in a repeating diamond-shaped pattern to stop bacteria from growing on us, so they've mimicked these denticles to create anti-fouling surfaces on their ships and submarines."

People say that he wrote the piece for Therese Malfatti, but he didn't. He wrote it for me – Elise.

He didn't write it for me because I was his muse. He wrote it for me because I didn't get the chance to write it down myself, as I got typhus and died. He didn't *consciously* know that he'd written it for me, though.

* * * * *

I decided to inhabit his dream because his other music was so exquisite, I knew that his arrangement of my piece would be exquisite, too.

In order to plant my tune into his dream, I'd needed to come up with a narrative, so I bumped into him in a park and introduced myself...then we got talking, and I started humming.

* * * * *

Ludwig woke, vaguely cognisant of a dream he'd had the night before, and he skipped over to his piano and played the following notes – ED ED EBDCA.

A few hours later, he finished writing his Bagatelle No. 25 in A Minor, and he decided to give his piece a second title – a lady's name that just happened to pop into his head.

* * * * *

On 27th April, 1810, Ludwig van Beethoven *literally* wrote for Elise.

Für Elise went on to become one of the most well-known pieces of classical music of all time.

201

Two pigs, a mouse, a worm, a camel and a fish entered a bar.

"My name's Carlyle," said the barman. "What can I get you?"

"A beer for me," said the first pig.

"And I just wish that I could stop itching," said the second pig.

Carlyle pulled a pint for the first pig and grabbed a packet of pork scratchings for the second.

"That was kind," squeaked the mouse. "Worm and I would like two absinthes, please."

"Are you really going to drink these?" asked Carlyle, pouring out the two very strong drinks.

"I reckon mouse will," said one of the pigs, "but worm won't, as he's got no backbone."

"And what can I get you two?" said Carlyle, addressing the camel and the fish.

"Two glasses of wine for us, please," said the camel.

"I'll get *you* a glass of wine," said Carlyle, "but not your friend."

"Why ever not?" asked the camel.

"Because your friend's clearly legless."

"And you, Carlyle, are Clearly mixed up," said the fish.

202

I slid down the flume and popped out at the bottom.

Fresh air at last.

"It's a boy!" said a woman in white. "What are you going to call him?"

"Elijah," cooed a woman who was lying on a bed

looking utterly exhausted.

Well, thanks very much, I thought. *Don't consult me, will you? I'm just the one who has to be known by the moniker for the rest of my life, so why get my input, eh?*

"Would you like to cut the navel string?" asked the lady in white.

Woah! You're going to cut that thing? It's attached to me! It could hurt!

"It won't hurt your wife or son," said the woman, passing a pair of scissors to a man who must have been my dad. "Umbilical cords don't contain any nerves."

Easy for you to say, lady. You're not the one with one sticking out of your belly button.

As my dad held the cord and brandished the scissors, I obviously had to voice my concerns, so I opened my mouth to query whether they were 100% sure that there would be no pain. However, all that came out of my oral cavity was a sort of strangulated screaming sound.

"There there, Elijah," said my dad, comforting me. "Don't worry. This won't hurt."

No dad! Don't do this to me!

But my dad cut the cord, and, fortunately, it didn't actually hurt.

You were lucky that that didn't hurt me. Now can you please clean me up? I'm covered in slime.

The woman in white could clearly understand me because she wiped me down, then placed me next to the lady who I assumed to be my mother, and my mother started crying.

Well, that's not the best of starts, is it? I was hoping you'd be pleased to see me?

"Oh he's so beautiful."

Talk about mixed messages.

"He looks just like you, Will."

Well, no, I don't, do I? For one, I'm much smaller; and, two, I don't have any hair or teeth. So I don't look like him at all.

"I don't know. He's got your nose, Marie."

An odd comment given my mum's nose was clearly on her face.

"If I could just prise Elijah away from you, Marie, and quickly check him over?"

The woman in white lifted me up, laid me on a blanket and started prodding me.

Was nothing sacred?

"I'm just going to pop you into this dish, Elijah."

Finally I was being consulted on what was happening to me.

"Nine pounds."

My God, were they going to sell me?

"I'm now going to give Elijah a shot of vitamin K, as discussed," said the woman, picking up an enormous needle.

What the heck?

"It's okay, Elijah," said my dad, stroking me.

Well, no, it's not okay, is it? You're not the one with a big scary needle heading your way.

"It'll soon be over," said the woman in white as she stabbed me.

I calmly explained to the woman that randomly stabbing people with needles was unethical, at best, and illegal, at worst, but all that came out of my mouth was a gurgling cry.

I could see that these next few months were going to be very trying.

203

"You cheated on me and told her you loved her! How could you?"

"I did not cheat on you or say anything to her. I haven't even seen her!"

"You did. Rebecca heard you."

"Why do you believe Rebecca but not me? Rebecca's just gossiping and repeating things."

"Exactly. She heard you say it."

"For God's sake, are you really going to believe Rebecca over me?"

"Yes. I trust Rebecca. Rebecca wouldn't make this up."

"She's just a stupid bird."

"Ugh, did you really just say that?"

"Yes, I did."

"Rebecca heard you tell Sky that you loved her – 'I love Sky'."

"Look, I do not love Sky, and I haven't seen Sky in ages."

"You never really got over her. I've always known that."

"I am totally over her!"

"And here I was stupidly looking forward to our trip to the Hebrides, when all the while you've been secretly canoodling with your ex."

"I have not been secretly canoodling with my ex! The last time I saw Sky was *months ago*."

"Lies. Rebecca heard you."

"Look, I don't know what Rebecca heard, as Sky's never set foot in this house, and I got Rebecca a long time after things ended with Sky."

"I don't believe anything that comes out of your mouth anymore. I'm off!"

She slammed the door.

"Oh Rebecca, what did you hear?" he said, looking at his parrot.

* * * * *

A couple of days earlier, he'd been standing by Rebecca's cage when he'd rung the holiday company.

"Hello, I'm just ringing about my upcoming trip to the

Isle of Skye."

204

It was their first day at school, and they were all feeling a little anxious. Would they get on with the other students? Would they be able to cope with the work? Would the teachers be nice?

They were sitting at their desks when their first teacher glided in.

"Welcome," sang the teacher. "I hope that you thoroughly enjoy your time at this school. My name's Hadraniel, and I'm going to teach you everything that there is to know about love. Love is the world's greatest healing force, and it really can transcend everything. So, if I can get you all to turn to page 32 of your green textbooks, together we can learn some more."

An hour and a half later, the class broke for recess – and, once recess was over, they congregated in the courtyard and waited for their physical education teacher to turn up.

"I'm Tabbris," said a teacher suddenly appearing and introducing himself to his new pupils. "If I could ask you all to board the bus that's waiting in the school car park, it'll take you down to the coast, where you'll be learning how to dive."

Twenty minutes later, the students alighted from the bus, and Tabbris asked them to stand in a line at the top of the cliff.

Once the students were all lined up, Tabbris jumped off the cliff, demonstrating how to make a smooth landing.

"Now you try!" he shouted from the bottom of the cliff.

That afternoon, the new pupils had one final class.

"I'm Linette," announced the pupils' third and final teacher of the day, "and I teach halo skills."

There was a murmur of excitement.

"It's a struggle, at first, to keep your halo levitating at the regulated five centimetres," said Linette, pointing to the circle of light a couple of inches above her head. "But, with time and practice, it'll become second nature to you."

205

"You're very up and down, Rook."

"I know, mate. I wish I was more like you; always looking forwards and never looking back."

"But I'm ten a penny. There're only two of you."

"But you're among people who understand you."

"Yes, that's true. The Knight's coming along in leaps and bounds, isn't he?"

"He is, mate. The King and Queen are still very directionless, though."

"Perhaps they need to spend some time with the Bishop – who, unlike you, Rook, isn't at all up and down."

"That's a good idea. I think the King should definitely spend some time with the Bishop, as I know that the thought of capture drives him mad."

"I wonder what their schedules say they're doing tomorrow."

"I don't know. I'll go and check, mate."

206

Howie and his best friend, Gordon – his mobile phone – walked into the city centre.

The city boasted a plethora of weird and wonderful museums, and while Howie was keen to explore the anthropological museum, Gordon wanted to visit the science and technology museum – so they went their separate ways, agreeing to reconvene a couple of hours later.

Howie walked into the anthropological museum and asked what exhibitions they had on that day, and there were two that particularly interested him – 'Amazonia' and 'Twenty-First Century Britain'.

After visiting the Amazonian exhibition – which featured intricate works of basketry and carvings that were used for ceremonial purposes – he made his way to the 'Twenty-First Century Britain' display, where he learnt that early twenty-first century Britons had had to work 40-hour weeks. He couldn't imagine having to work such long hours, but seeing how basic the twenty-first-century technology had been, he could understand why the early Britons had had to.

Over at the science and technology museum, Gordon had made his way to the mobile phone exhibition, where he learnt that the first widely-available mobile phones were just rectangular hunks of plastic that could only be used to make phone calls. They had absolutely no awareness, consciousness or intelligence whatsoever. Gordon marvelled at how basic and inanimate they were, and he lamented the fact that they would have had absolutely no quality of life whatsoever. They couldn't think, and they couldn't move.

A couple of hours later, Howie and Gordon reconvened, realising just how lucky they were to live in modern times.

207

Garage sale: door, walls, ceiling, floor.

The big day arrived, and Neville hoped it would go well, as being able to drive would give him his independence and he'd no longer be reliant on the taxi service of mum and dad.

He walked into the test centre and gave the receptionist his provisional licence and theory test certificate, and she took the documents and told him to take a seat.

Nerves affect people in different ways, and Neville's nerves manifested in the form of excessive fidgeting. However, he was soon put out of his misery when the receptionist told him to go outside to the car park, where the examiner would be waiting for him.

He walked out of the test centre and made a beeline for his instructor's car, which was parked at the far end of the car park. His instructor had decided to wait in a nearby café for the duration of his test.

"I'm Jonny," said a man suddenly appearing.

"Neville," said Neville, shaking Jonny's hand.

"The first thing that I want you to do," said Jonny, "is read the number plate on the red car that's parked next to the white van."

"GX65 FVQ," said Neville.

"Good," said Jonny. "We always begin by checking our candidates' eye-sights. Now, if you can jump into your car, please, Neville, we'll begin the test."

As Neville opened the driver's door and sat in the driver's seat, Jonny jumped into the passenger seat.

"We're now going to start your test," said Jonny, clutching a clipboard. "So, if you can drive out of the car park and take a left, please, Neville?"

Neville reversed out of the parking bay and exited the car park, remembering to keep his hands in a ten-to-two position.

"So, what do you do for a living, Neville?" asked Jonny.

"I'm a trainee chef," said Neville, thinking that Jonny was assessing whether he was capable of talking while driving.

"Oh, very good," said Jonny. "Can you take the second right, please, just after the postbox?"

Neville took the second right as instructed.

"I'd now like you to pull up somewhere on the left, please, Neville, as I'm going to ask you to perform a manoeuvre."

Neville found a suitable spot and parked up, praying that he'd be asked to do either a three-point turn or a reverse round a corner, as his parallel parks were a bit hit-and-miss.

"Right," said Jonny. "I'd now like you to do a doughnut."

"Do a doughnut?" repeated Neville, astounded.

"Yes, please, Neville. Give it your best shot."

"But–" began Neville.

"Now, please, Neville."

Neville indicated right, looked over his shoulder and started driving down the empty road, then he turned the steering wheel sharply to his right and rammed down the throttle, and the car span around beautifully.

"Good," enthused Jonny. "Good. There was just a bit of oversteer when driving out of it."

"That was amazing," gasped Neville. "It felt so good!"

"Keep driving forwards, please, Neville, and when you get to the junction, I'd like you to turn left and join the A road."

Neville joined the A road and quickly built up his speed to 60mph.

"Right," said Jonny. "I'd now like to test your racing skills."

"Test my racing skills?" said Neville, agog.

"Yes, Neville, your racing skills. So, in your own time, I'd like you to increase your speed to triple figures, please."

"Triple figures?" stuttered Neville.

"Yes, Neville, triple figures."

Neville put his foot down and watched the needle on the speedometer shift to the right.

"Good, good," said Jonny as Neville hit three digits.

The sirens were faint to begin with, then they got louder and louder.

The police car was right behind them.

"I guess I need to pull over?" said Neville.

"I guess you do," agreed Jonny.

Neville pulled into a lay-by, and the police car tucked in behind him.

"Afternoon," said the policeman as Neville wound down his car window.

"Afternoon," said Neville, shakily.

The police officer seemed a bit taken aback for a minute, then continued with his line of questioning.

"Our radar shows that you were driving at 104mph – 44mph above the national speed limit. This is an extremely serious offence and will almost definitely result in a disqualification. Do you have anything to say?"

"My driving test examiner told me to do it," squeaked Neville.

"What examiner?" asked the police officer.

"My driving test examiner – Jonny," said Neville, pointing to his left.

"Young man, do not make matters worse for yourself here, please."

As the policeman dragged Neville out of his car and into the back of the police car, Neville felt incredibly confused.

* * * * *

"I've never been so ashamed in all my life," thundered Neville's dad. "To think that a child of mine would take out a car without a supervisor – *on the day of his test* – and drive in such a dangerous and reckless manner. It's so humiliating. You're a disgrace to this family."

"But–", whimpered Neville.

"And," continued Neville's dad, ignoring his son, "to add insult to injury, you claim that a *non-existent examiner* told you to do it. You are grounded indefinitely, young man, and goodness only knows what will happen to you at your court hearing."

Neville and his father left the police station, and Neville wondered whether he ought to see a psychiatrist.

* * * * *

"He's done it again," whispered the police officer who'd brought Neville in.

"Jonny?" asked a second police officer.

"Yes."

"We can't keep protecting him like this."

"I know, but he was our colleague, and he's our friend."

"It's not fair on the kids."

"I know."

"They lose their learner licences and probably think that they've lost their marbles, too."

"I know, although they should know better than to do doughnuts and drive at break-neck speeds just because someone tells them to."

"But they're young, and the young find it hard to stand up to authority figures. Well, *alleged* authority figures."

"So what do we do? We can't keep covering for Jonny, but we can't dob him in, either. Not after the appalling way he was treated. They completely broke him."

"I know. I think he just wants to waste police time, and who can blame him?"

209

She'd always had a fascination with buttons – the sort you pressed, not the fasteners on clothes. This fascination had begun when she was little and would go to museums with her mum, dad and brother. Some of the museums had featured interactive displays, and she'd loved to press, twist and slide the displays' buttons, dials and sliders. Her dad would often joke that she was more interested in pressing the buttons than in understanding what the displays were trying to show her.

* * * * *

She first met Mark when she was 16. She saw him playing guitar on stage and knew that she wanted to get to know him. So she did. And their relationship blossomed.

When Mark was 18, he and his bandmates won a prize to spend some time in a recording studio, and he asked her to go with them.

As she walked into the studio with Mark and the other Flying Rats, the hairs on the back of her neck stood up, and as Mark and the Rats started to unpack their kit in the live room, she walked into the control room and her jaw dropped.

She'd never seen such a big mixing console before – a vast array of buttons, dials and sliders that could adjust the volumes, timbres and dynamics of the different audio signals.

In that moment, she knew what she wanted to do with the rest of her life.

Dear Cardiff,

How are you?

Everything's okay here, although I've been feeling quite full of late, but that's because it's nearly Christmas. I guess it's been the same for you?

Best wishes, Bristol

Dear Bristol,

Thanks for the letter, and I'm happy to report that I'm well, thanks.

I know what you mean about feeling full! I've been feeling this way for a few weeks now, but at least we know we'll quickly lose weight after Christmas. I quite like Christmas, though, as it's the one time of the year when I really feel needed. I don't know about you, but I've started to feel a bit redundant the rest of the year.

Best wishes, Cardiff

Dear Cardiff,

I know what you mean about feeling redundant apart from at Christmas, and I worry that one day we won't be needed at all. Let's hope that won't be for a good few years yet, though. Talking of Christmas, I trust you had a good one?

It's very cold, isn't it? Roll on spring.

Best wishes, Bristol

Dear Bristol,

How wonderful it is to be outdoors now that spring has sprung.

All's good my end, although I had a rather unpleasant time a few nights ago when a drunken youth urinated up me. I do wish that people would show us some respect.

Speak soon.
Best wishes, Cardiff

Dear Cardiff,

It was good to hear from you, and I do sympathise over your unpleasant ordeal because I had a similar thing happen to me last year, which was not nice. It's as disagreeable as having someone scrawl some vulgarity across you.

Keep enjoying the lovely weather and the light evenings.

Best wishes, Bristol

Dear Bristol,

The most bizarre thing has happened to me! I've been painted gold! A local cyclist did well at the Olympics, so I was painted gold in her honour. I'm not sure how I feel about it to be honest. It's nice to have a fresh lick of paint, but…gold? It's extremely flashy and so very different to being red.

Best wishes, Cardiff

211

"Tuck me in," said Frankie.

"Alright," said Frankie's dad, walking over to his son's bed.

"And will you tell me a story?"

"I will, but only if you promise to do your tuba practice tomorrow."

Frankie's music teacher had told Frankie's dad, Paul, that Frankie had a natural talent for tuba but struggled to apply himself and commit to his practice. So, not wanting his son's talent to go to waste, Paul was keen to encourage Frankie to practice more.

"Alright, I'll do my practice," groaned Frankie. "Now

can I have my story?"

"Okay," said Paul, hurriedly trying to think up a story.

"Great!" sang Frankie.

"Being in an orchestra was really good fun," began Paul, a cunning plan formulating in his mind, "and Terence the Tuba got to play in concert halls all over the world, accompanied by his best friends Timmy the Trombone and Heather the Horn. However, Terence was curious, daring and brave and was always wanting more excitement and new adventures – his friends in the woodwind section said that he was as bold as brass."

Paul noticed his wife, Lilia, standing in the doorway, and he saw her quietly snigger at his terrible pun.

"So, when Terence's orchestra was asked to play at the rocket launch, Terence was thrilled, as meeting real-life astronauts and seeing a rocket blast off into space was a super exciting adventure.

"It was also a super exciting adventure for Daniel the Drum, who wouldn't stop banging on about it."

"Wow," enthused Frankie.

Lilia stifled another giggle and rolled her eyes.

"As the rocket launch drew near," continued Paul, "Terence practised and practised his music, as he didn't want to make any mistakes on the big day."

"Very wise," said Frankie.

"He also thought that it would be fun to decorate his case for the event, so he, Timmy and Heather went shopping for some space stickers.

"On the evening before the launch, Terence tucked himself up inside his case, and he slept, and he slept, and he slept, and he slept, as he was very tired from all of his practicing.

"On waking up the next day, he climbed out of his case and was surprised to find that he was very light on his feet – so much so, he realised he was floating! He was very confused, so he looked around for Timmy, Heather and Daniel to see if they could shed some light on the situation.

But they were nowhere to be seen. There were, however, two humans floating around him, and the humans were staring at him, agog.

"'How on earth did a tuba end up on the station?' marvelled one of the humans.

"'That's a funny turn of phrase,' replied the other, 'given we're not on Earth.'

"*Blow me,* thought Terence the Tuba. *I'm in space. I'm actually in space!*

"After Terence had tucked himself up in his case the night before the rocket launch, he'd overslept and hadn't got up and out of his case the next morning, so the people who were packing the rocket must have seen his case – which was covered in space stickers – and packed it onto the rocket."

"Oh wow!" said Frankie. "So Terence got to go to space!"

"He did, son," said Paul. "Over the next few days, Terence got used to living in a zero-gravity environment, and he learnt how to do flips, twists, somersaults, turns, twirls and whirls. He'd often gaze down at Earth and wonder what Timmy, Heather and Daniel would think if they could see him spinning around, having such a great adventure.

"Back on Earth, Timmy, Heather and Daniel were very worried about Terence, so they raised their concerns with the orchestra's top brass, who launched a missing tuba campaign."

Lilia giggled again, and Paul winked at her.

"Posters were made," continued Paul, "displaying Terence's name and photograph and asking people to contact the orchestra if they saw him.

"In order to take their minds off their worry, Timmy and Heather played duets, and Daniel watched the astronauts' vlogs, which were broadcast live from the space station…and it was while watching one of these vlogs that Daniel almost jumped out of his skin."

"Very clever, honey," smiled Lilia.

"Why did Daniel the Drum almost jump out of his skin, daddy?" asked Frankie.

"Well, son, Daniel noticed something large, shiny and gold bobbing about behind one of the astronauts. 'Is that…no, it can't be…' he muttered. Then, as clear as day, Terence the Tuba floated out in front of the astronaut.

"Daniel's heart skipped a beat, and he cried out, 'Timmy, Heather – come and look at this! Terence is in space! Terence is in space!'

"Timmy and Heather rushed over to Daniel, looked at his computer screen and couldn't believe their eyes.

"'Good gracious!' bellowed Timmy, 'Terence is an astro-tuba!'

"The news of Terence's whereabouts travelled fast, and everyone in the orchestra was very excited for him – so much so, many a rehearsal would end with the orchestra watching the latest astronaut vlog on a specially-installed big screen; all of the instruments wanting to catch a glimpse of Terence. And it was at the end of one particular rehearsal, and during one of the astronaut's live vlogs, that something incredible happened…

"The astronaut was about to go on a spacewalk and was showing his viewers the tether attached to his spacesuit, which had a clip at the end of it that had to be fastened to the side of the space station at all times so he wouldn't float away.

"The orchestra saw Terence suddenly float into view, and they all cheered. The cymbals clapped."

Lilia groaned.

"The astronaut opened the space station door," continued Paul, "and was about to clip the end of his tether to the side of the space station when Terence let out a very loud, and very long, blast.

"The startled astronaut floated back into the space station and shut the door, perplexed, and one of the other astronauts floated up to him and quickly realised why

Terence had set off an alarm. 'The clip on the end of your tether is loose!' she exclaimed, horrified. 'Had you gone on your spacewalk, you'd never have come back!'

"'Gracious,' exclaimed the shocked spacewalker. 'That tuba just saved my life.'

"The orchestra, who'd been watching with bated breath, realised that Terence – who their conductor often said was very sharp – must have spotted the loose clip and made a loud sound to stop the astronaut from leaving the station. Terence was a hero, and the instruments were all very proud of him."

"Wow," gasped Frankie.

"Terence isn't the only one who's very sharp," giggled Lilia.

"Over the next few weeks, the story of Terence the Tuba accidentally going to space and saving an astronaut's life really struck a chord. It was a fantastic good news story, and Terence appeared on the front of many newspapers.

"When Terence returned to Earth a few weeks' later, he was asked to attend a lot of parties, and he'd always take Daniel the Drum with him, as Daniel liked a big bash."

"Oh Paul," said Lilia, rolling her eyes. "Although great story. But the puns! No!"

"So Terence the Tuba was a hero…and he got to go to space!" chirruped Frankie.

"He was, and he did, son," said Paul. "Now give me and mummy a kiss, and then it's bedtime for you, young man."

The next morning, Paul and Lilia were sitting at the breakfast bar eating their cereal when they heard a loud, rumbling sound coming from upstairs.

"What's that?" said Paul, alarmed.

"It's Frankie practising his tuba," said Lilia, her eyes sparkling.

"Ah, good on you, Terence," grinned Paul.

212

This was it. His final hour.

He was surrounded by his wife, Beryl, and their two grown-up children, and he asked to speak to each of them in turn.

He told his elder child, Kellie, how proud he was of her because she'd followed in his footsteps and pursued a medical career; and he told his younger child, Stan, who was trying to carve out a career as a sculptor, to keep following his dreams because the definition of success was spending your life doing something you loved.

With Beryl, words weren't needed. They just hugged.

And, then, suddenly, Ted appeared...although Beryl couldn't see him.

"Are you ready, Patrick?"

"I am, Ted."

213

Suki got into her car and began the hour-long commute to work, knowing that the only person who could cheer her up on a Monday morning was Justin Bowles.

DJ Justin Bowles had been broadcasting for about an hour when the gunman entered the green room, tied the two singers to the table and wrote something on a piece of paper, which he held up against the glass partition so Justin could see it in his studio.

Keep broadcasting and don't get help, else the singers will be shot.

The gunman then dropped the piece of paper, pointed his gun at Justin's guests and stared at Justin through the glass divide.

The song that was playing on the radio show was nearing its conclusion, so Justin knew he had just seconds to compose himself in order to appear normal to his listeners.

"Well, I hope you enjoyed that," he said, his voice wobbling a little. "And it sure was an appropriate song for a Monday morning. 'Manic Monday' was the first single to be released from the Bangles' second studio album – 'Different Light'."

"The Bangles were great," muttered Suki, turning up the volume on her car radio and thinking that Justin sounded a bit 'off'.

"Next up on Storm FM is Queen's 'Bohemian Rhapsody'."

As Justin set the song spinning – the longest song he could think of – he knew he had six minutes of thinking time.

What do I do? I can't ring, or text, the police, as the gunman's watching my every move – he'd be on to me straight away. And I can't leave the studio, else he'd shoot Jerry and Peggy. So I need to send an SOS message without him knowing. But how do I do that?

And then he had an idea…but he knew it was a long shot.

"That was 'Bohemian Rhapsody' by Queen."

Tune, thought Suki.

"Next up on Storm FM is 'Help' by the Beatles. John Lennon said he wrote 'Help' because being in the Beatles was so overwhelming he was subconsciously crying out for *help*."

The way that Justin stressed the word 'help' made Suki furrow her brow in concern, but then she was a psychiatrist, so she was probably just over-analysing things.

"It's Monday 3rd October, and you're listening to DJ Bowles here at Storm FM," said Justin as 'Help' ended and he set the next track spinning. As the track played, he glanced up at the glass partition and locked eyes with the

210

gunman, which sent a shiver down his spine.

"That was 'Human' by the *Killers* here at Storm FM. 'Human' was the third Killers song to make it into the UK top five, and it was released as the first single from their 2009 studio album, 'Day & Age'."

Justin definitely just stressed the word 'killers', thought Suki. *I'm sure I'm not imagining it. And why isn't he being his usual hilarious self today? Why all this musical trivia?*

"This is Storm FM, and the time is now 8.24 on Monday 3rd October, and that was *'Hostage'* by the Australian singer, Sia. Sia, who's known for covering up her face, wrote 'Hostage' with Nick Valensi as part of her sixth studio album – '1,000 Forms of Fear'."

I'm definitely not imagining it now, thought Suki. *There's something up. It was subtle, but Justin had just emphasised the word 'hostage' like he had the words 'help' and 'killers'. And he's definitely not his usual self today – he's gone from irreverent jack-the-lad to walking pop encyclopaedia. I need to pull over and do something.*

As Suki kept driving, impatient for a lay-by, Justin set the next track spinning.

"It's Monday morning, and you're listening to Justin Bowles here at Storm FM, and that was 'Message in a Bottle' by the *Police*."

The gunman arched his eyebrow, and Justin realised that he needed to throw him off the scent.

"Now, not many of you will know this, but it's 'National Boyfriend Day' today, so this next song's for all you boyfriends out there."

Suki finally came to a lay-by and pulled into it. She grabbed her mobile phone and dialled 999, and, on connecting with the police, shared her fear that something was awry at Storm FM. She said that it was just a hunch, but as an experienced psychiatrist, it was a hunch that she strongly suggested the police explore.

Thirty minutes later, as 'Code' by British electronica band Faithless was spinning, the police pulled up into the

Storm FM car park.

214

"I covered 12,000 miles in one day, which is twenty times the distance from Land's End to John O'Groats as the crow flies."

"You sure can move," said the skin to the blood.

215

01001001   00100000   01101100   01101111

01110110   01100101   00100000

01111001   01101111   01110101   00101110

00100000   01001001   00100000

01100011   01100001   01101110   00100000

01100110   01100101   01100101

01101100 00100000 01101100 01101111

01110110 01100101 00101110

216

It was time for their assessment.
"Some of you are sharp.
"Some of you are strong.
"And some of you are wise," said the dentist.

217

"Your job is definitely more exciting than mine – you don't have to stand around as much as I do."

"But you get to wear nice clothes, whereas I'm always naked and barely a day goes by where I'm not involved in some sort of horrific car crash."

"We're clearly both dummies for doing these jobs."

It's uncommon to get to your 80s without having succumbed to at least one type of ailment - so, at 82, I felt blessed. Perhaps I'd remained disease-free because I'd led such an active, wholesome life, or maybe I was just incredibly lucky. My father always said that I was the luckiest person he knew. However, that luck finally ran out on my 83rd birthday. Or so I thought...

I hadn't wanted a fuss for my birthday, but my family had, so the village hall was hired and decorated, and we had a party.

It was while blowing out my 83 candles that I felt a bit funny. As you get older, you lose lung capacity - but you need that lung capacity to blow out your ever-increasing number of birthday candles. So I put the strange tingling feeling that I had in my left arm down to over-exertion from candle blowing. However, the tingling feeling crept up my body to my face, and the next thing I knew I was lying on the floor with a sea of concerned faces staring down at me.

Thanks to my quick-thinking daughter, who suspected it was a stroke and called the ambulance straight away, I didn't die. I did lose the ability to use my right hand, though - which, as a right-handed author, was rather a blow. Where there's a will there's a way, though, so I reasoned that I still had a fully-functioning left hand, so I'd jolly well use that instead. However, I'm not ambidextrous, so when I first tried writing with my left hand, I knew that it would be frustrating and difficult. What I didn't expect, though, was that I'd write the wrong way round!

When I raised this strange mirror-writing phenomenon with my doctor, I learnt that it wasn't as strange as I'd thought - apparently, mirror-writing isn't uncommon after having a stroke that's damaged your brain's left hemisphere.

I'm now 85, and just last year had my fifteenth novel published. It was a joint effort with my grandson, Petey. Petey had decided to take a gap year between school and university but needed money to travel, so I paid him to be my transcriber.

After writing each chapter, I'd pass my scribblings over to Petey, who would hold my words up to a mirror and type them out the right way round. It was a joy to spend so much time with my grandson, and he clearly developed an appetite for writing because he told me that he was going to try to write a book about his imminent travels. None of my children had ever shown any interest in writing, so to see my grandson develop an interest was heart-warming - and, in that moment, I realised that I was still an incredibly lucky person because even my stroke had been a stroke of luck.

219

"Everyone wanted me in the eighties and nineties," said Rebecca, "but not anymore."

"I feel for you, Rebecca," said James, who was fortunate to have always been popular.

"As do I," said Harry. "But, remember, Rebecca, anyone can make a comeback. Look what happened to me!"

"And me," said Florence.

"And me," added George.

"Don't give Rebecca false hope," said Edith. "Like you three, I was also incredibly popular at the turn of the century, but I'm not anymore."

"I'm sure your day will come, Edith," said Florence.

"Oh do shut up," growled Edith. "I've no desire to be mutton dressed up as lamb."

"Stop it, Edith," scolded Rebecca, "you're giving yourself a bad name."

220

"What's up, SM?" he asked, sensing she was down.

"I don't know. I guess I'm worried I'm not doing very much with my life and I'm not making much of a difference."

"Are you serious?" said FS. "You're doing great things; you give people a voice. Me, on the other hand, I'm the one at a dead end."

"Don't do yourself down," said SM.

"But lots of people do use me."

"That's true," said SM sympathetically.

"Stop feeling sorry for yourself, FS," said S, joining in the conversation. "Yes, you get used a lot, but imagine being me; I'm pretty much expendable to most people."

"Oh shut up, S," growled FS. "Did I ask for your opinion?"

"Pipe down both of you," interjected C, who was always breaking things up.

"Oh do let them keep going; it's funny," said EM, who liked it when people got animated.

"If there's going to be a contest about who gets treated the worst, I'd win hands down," said A.

"That's true," agreed the others.

"I'm used and abused more than any of you."

"Does it bother you?" asked QM, who was always wanting to know more.

"It does," sniffed A, starting to sob.

Speech mark, full stop, semicolon, comma, exclamation mark and question mark all went quiet, feeling apostrophe's pain.

221

First words: 222, 20, 85, 154, 7, 82

222

Linette's secondment to planet Earth had been very productive, and the earthlings had come to know her as 'Lady Luck'. However, in reality, she was just the Angel Linette from Gabriellium.

Some of Linette's good deeds included:

- Exposing the beauty of whale song;
- Ensuring that young, prodigious dancers heard the words of encouragement that they needed to

hear in order to believe in themselves and go on to achieve great things;

- Ensuring that footballers who thought that the weight of the world was on their shoulders realised that, while what they were doing *was* important, it wasn't that important;
- Ensuring that pets had doting owners;
- Ensuring that dying children had inspiring, kind doctors;
- Ensuring that scatty teenage babysitters – who would go on to do job interviews while painted green – had sensible mothers;
- Ensuring that people who lost their way met people who'd help pick them back up;
- Encouraging animals to stand up for themselves and have more of a voice;
- Ensuring people met their soulmates;
- Keeping the mantlers safe;
- Helping people discover their next big challenges, such as standing on every piece of the world's largest jigsaw puzzle;
- Blessing foetuses with the gift of contentment;
- Ensuring that running race water stations were positioned near churches with helpful vicars;
- Ensuring that pet owners were aware of paradoxes;
- Ensuring that people had friends who made them realise just how lucky they were;
- Ensuring that actors had quick-thinking stage manager wives;
- Ensuring that quick-thinking, technology-savvy people were in the audiences of plays;
- Ensuring that babies had wise, and slightly nutty, godparents;

- Ensuring that statues had the chance to see the positive difference they'd made;
- Ensuring that people in isolated homes had wonderful postmen;
- Giving troubled young children a link to the angels at Gabriellium via their snazzy headphones;
- Ensuring that people had dreams that would help keep them alive in subsequent real-life situations;
- Ensuring that overwhelmed parents had excellent friends;
- Ensuring that CCTV cameras were in the right place at the right time;
- Allowing the dead to allay the livings' fear of dying;
- Ensuring that quick-thinking baristas and psychiatrists were in the right places at the right times;
- Ensuring that students had memorable lecturers, and vice versa;
- Ensuring that animal lovers were present when whales needed them;
- Ensuring that brilliant young immunologists ignored their doubters;
- Giving people inspiration in life and death situations;
- Linking old people with young people who made them feel relevant again;
- Giving people functioning memories;
- Bringing dead people's creations to life through living people;
- Teaching halo skills at angel school;
- Helping people discover their vocations;
- Helping people see negatives as positives.

Angel Linette was sad that she hadn't had the capacity to help even more earthlings, such as:

- The morally-questionable tooth fairy;
- The young, prodigious dancer who didn't hear any words of encouragement;
- The couple who happened to be on the faulty plane;
- The two young mothers who thought the grass was always greener;
- The young boy who flew too close to the sun because he hadn't properly heard a key instruction;
- The refugee who had to endure the cruise passenger's first world problems;
- The unappreciated shopping trolley;
- The two men who lost their lives on the A272;
- The child genius who was paired with the narrow-minded teacher;
- The woman with dementia who thought it was her friend who had the disease;
- The young, Lego-loving boy with the horrid disease;
- The school children – then electorates – who had to put up with megalomaniacal leadership;
- The teddy bear with the stitched-up mouth;
- The non-returning explorers;
- The young man in the imbalanced friendship;
- The man who lost his wife, then pushed his daughter away;
- The spoilt child;
- The used and abused toilet door handle;
- The families who would have become lovers and friends had it not been for the war;
- The human who couldn't forgive the trees;

- The insomniac;
- The wise man who was shot by the intolerant man;
- The seer who was dismissed by the authorities;
- The humans who were players in the extra-terrestrial board game;
- The tiger that escaped from the zoo;
- The human the tiger ate;
- The man who had nightmares about the mundanity of the corporate world;
- The unempowered dolls;
- The spider whose masterpiece was destroyed;
- The well-intentioned, law-breaking child;
- The goalless ex-sportswoman;
- The employees who were being spied on;
- The woman who was eaten by the Kathrokas;
- The woman's daughter, who was enrolled on the Kathrokas' breeding programme;
- The sick woman with the judgmental colleague;
- The victims of the hurricane;
- The good forces that couldn't balance out their opposing bad forces;
- The woman who lost her life while seizing life;
- The unempowered puppet;
- The Jewish girl whose whereabouts were revealed;
- The man with the garrulous parrot;
- The disgruntled, ill-treated police officer;
- The young man with the dubious driving instructor;
- The postboxes that were worried they were going to become redundant;
- The unloved computer;
- The once-fashionable names;

- The abused apostrophe.

Angel Linette wished she could tell these earthlings that she would have loved to have helped them, too.

Printed in Great Britain
by Amazon

36658011R00128